Praise for Jeffrey Archer's short stories

'Somerset Maugham never penned anything so swift or urbanely witty as this'   *Publishers Weekly*

'Outstanding . . . white-knuckle suspense and witty denouements. Enjoyable, suspense-filled rival to Roald Dahl'
Daily Express

'Stylish, witty and constantly entertaining . . . Jeffrey Archer has a natural aptitude for short stories'   *The Times*

'Jeffrey Archer plays a subtle cat-and-mouse game with the reader in twelve original short stories that end, more often than not, with our collective whiskers twitching in surprise'
New York Times

'Archer hits the bull's eye with an exemplary collection'
Daily Mail

'The economy and precision of Archer's prose never fails to delight. The criminal doesn't always get away with his crime and justice doesn't always prevail, but the reader wins with each and every story'   *Publishers Weekly*

'I was reading the book on tour and found I was bunking off from my own signing sessions to get back to the story. Sitting in a Starbucks in Oxford, feverishly thumbing the pages to find out what dire machinations Hugo Barrington (a villain straight out of Victorian melodrama) would come up with next, I had to admit I was utterly hooked. It was an absurdly enjoyable read' Anthony Horowitz, *Daily Telegraph*

'This is going to be huge. It looks terrific, it is terrific'
Bookseller, paperback preview

Praise for Jeffrey Archer's novels

'If there was a Nobel prize for storytelling, Archer would win'
Daily Telegraph

'Probably the greatest storyteller of our age' *Mail on Sunday*

'The man's a genius . . . the strength and excitement of the idea carries all before it' *Evening Standard*

'A storyteller in the class of Alexandre Dumas' *Washington Post*

'Archer has a gift for storytelling that can only be described as genius' *Daily Telegraph*

'Back in top form . . . Archer's imagination at its most sublime . . . an entertaining, pacey page-turner' *Sunday Times*

'Few are more famous than Archer for keeping the pages turning . . . an extravagant romp – possibly his best' *The Times*

A TWIST IN THE TALE

JEFFREY ARCHER, whose novels and short stories include *Kane and Abel*, *A Prisoner of Birth* and *Cat O' Nine Tales*, has topped the bestseller lists around the world, with sales of over 270 million copies.

He is the only author ever to have been a number one bestseller in fiction (seventeen times), short stories (four times) and non-fiction (*The Prison Diaries*).

The author is married with two sons and lives in London and Cambridge.

www.jeffreyarcher.com

Facebook.com/JeffreyArcherAuthor

@Jeffrey_Archer

ALSO BY JEFFREY ARCHER

JEFFREY ARCHER

A TWIST IN THE TALE

PAN BOOKS

First published 1988 by Hodder & Stoughton Ltd

First published by Pan Books 2003

This edition published 2014 by Pan Books
an imprint of Pan Macmillan, a division of Macmillan Publishers Limited
Pan Macmillan, 20 New Wharf Road, London N1 9RR
Basingstoke and Oxford
Associated companies throughout the world
www.panmacmillan.com

ISBN 978-1-5098-0842-7

1 3 5 7 9 8 6 4 2

A CIP catalogue record for this book is available from the British Library.

Typeset by SetSystems Ltd, Saffron Walden, Essex
Printed and bound by CPI Group (UK) Ltd, Croydon, CR0 4YY

Visit **www.panmacmillan.com** to read more about all our books
and to buy them. You will also find features, author interviews and
news of any author events, and you can sign up for e-newsletters
so that you're always first to hear about our new releases.

To Henry and Suzanne

AUTHOR'S NOTE

Of these twelve short stories, gathered in my travels from Tokyo to Trumpington, ten are based on known incidents – some embellished with considerable licence. Only two are totally the result of my own imagination.

I would like to thank all those people who allowed me to learn some of their innermost secrets.

J. A.
September 1988

Contents

THE PERFECT MURDER

IF I HADN'T CHANGED my mind that night I would never have found out the truth.

I couldn't believe that Carla had slept with another man, that she had lied about her love for me – and that I might be second or even third in her affections.

Carla had phoned me at the office during the day, something I had told her not to do, but since I also warned her never to call me at home she hadn't been left with a lot of choice. As it turned out, all she had wanted to let me know was that she wouldn't be able to make it for what the French so decorously call a '*cinq à sept*'. She had to visit her sister in Fulham who had been taken ill, she explained.

I was disappointed. It had been another depressing day, and now I was being asked to forgo the one thing that would have made it bearable.

'I thought you didn't get on well with your sister,' I said tartly.

There was no immediate reply from the other end. Eventually Carla asked, 'Shall we make it next Tuesday, the usual time?'

'I don't know if that's convenient,' I said. 'I'll call

you on Monday when I know what my plans are.' I put down the receiver.

Wearily, I phoned my wife to let her know I was on the way home – something I usually did from the phone box outside Carla's flat. It was a trick I often used to make Elizabeth feel she knew where I was every moment of the day.

Most of the office staff had already left for the night so I gathered together some papers I could work on at home. Since the new company had taken us over six months ago, the management had not only sacked my Number Two in the accounts department but expected me to cover his work as well as my own. I was hardly in a position to complain, since my new boss made it abundantly clear that if I didn't like the arrangement I should feel free to seek employment elsewhere. I might have, too, but I couldn't think of many firms that would readily take on a man who had reached that magic age somewhere between the sought-after and the available.

As I drove out of the office car park and joined the evening rush hour I began to regret having been so sharp with Carla. After all, the role of the other woman was hardly one she delighted in. The feeling of guilt persisted, so that when I reached the corner of Sloane Square, I jumped out of my car and ran across the road.

'A dozen roses,' I said, fumbling with my wallet.

A man who must have made his profit from lovers selected twelve unopened buds without comment. My choice didn't show a great deal of imagination but at least Carla would know I'd tried.

I drove on towards her flat, hoping she had not yet left for her sister's, that perhaps we might even find time for a quick drink. Then I remembered that I had already told my wife I was on the way home. A few minutes' delay could be explained by a traffic jam, but that lame excuse could hardly cover my staying on for a drink.

When I arrived at Carla's home I had the usual trouble finding a parking space, until I spotted a gap that would just take a Rover opposite the paper shop. I stopped and would have backed into the space had I not noticed a man coming out of the entrance to her block of flats. I wouldn't have given it a second thought if Carla hadn't followed him a moment later. She stood there in the doorway, wearing a loose blue housecoat. She leaned forward to give her departing visitor a kiss that could hardly have been described as sisterly. As she closed the door I drove my car round the corner and double-parked.

I watched the man in my rear-view mirror as he crossed the road, went into the newsagent and a few moments later reappeared with an evening paper and what looked like a packet of cigarettes. He walked to his car, a blue BMW, stopped to remove a parking ticket from his windscreen and appeared to curse. How long had the BMW been there? I even began to wonder if he had been with Carla when she phoned to tell me not to come round.

The man climbed into the BMW, fastened his seat belt and lit a cigarette before driving off. I took his parking meter space in part-payment for my woman. I didn't consider it a fair exchange. I checked up and down the street, as I always did, before getting out and walking over to the block of flats. It was already dark and no one gave me a second glance. I pressed the bell marked 'Moorland'.

When Carla opened the front door I was greeted with a huge smile which quickly turned into a frown, then just as quickly back to a smile. The first smile must have been meant for the BMW man. I often wondered why she wouldn't give me a front-door key. I stared into those blue eyes that had first captivated me so many months ago. Despite her smile, those eyes now revealed a coldness I had never seen before.

She turned to re-open the door and let me into her ground-floor flat. I noticed that under her house-coat she was wearing the wine-red negligee I had given her for Christmas. Once inside the flat I found myself checking round the room I knew so well. On the glass table in the centre of the room stood the 'Snoopy' coffee mug I usually drank from, empty. By its side was Carla's mug, also empty, and a dozen roses arranged in a vase. The buds were just beginning to open.

I have always been quick to chide and the sight of the flowers made it impossible for me to hide my anger.

'And who was the man who just left?' I asked.

'An insurance broker,' she replied, removing the mugs from the table.

'And what was he insuring?' I asked. 'Your love-life?'

'Why do you automatically assume he's my lover?' Her voice had begun to rise.

'Do you usually have coffee with an insurance broker in your negligee? Come to think of it, *my* negligee.'

'I'll have coffee with whom I damn well please,' she said, 'and wearing what I damn well please, especially when you are on your way home to your wife.'

'But I had wanted to come to you –'

'And then return to your wife. In any case, you're always telling me I should lead my own life and not rely on you,' she added, an argument Carla often fell back on when she had something to hide.

'You know it's not that easy.'

'I know it's easy enough for you to jump into bed with me whenever it suits you. That's all I'm good for, isn't it?'

'That's not fair.'

'Not fair? Weren't you hoping for your usual at six so you could still be home at seven in time for supper with Elizabeth?'

'I haven't made love to my wife in years!' I shouted.

'We only have your word for that,' she spat out with scorn.

'I have been utterly faithful to you.'

'Which means I always have to be to you, I suppose?'

'Stop behaving like a whore.'

Carla's eyes flashed as she leaped forward and slapped me across the face with all the strength she could muster.

I was still slightly off-balance when she raised her arm a second time, but as her hand came swinging towards me I blocked it and was even able to push her back against the mantelpiece. She recovered quickly and came flying at me again.

In a moment of uncontrolled fury, just as she was about to launch herself on me, I clenched my fist and took a swing at her. I caught her on the side of the chin, and she wheeled back from the impact. I watched her put an arm out to break her fall. But before she had the chance to leap back up and retaliate, I turned and strode out, slamming the flat door behind me.

I ran down the hall, out on to the street, jumped into my car and drove off quickly. I couldn't have been with her for more than ten minutes. Although I felt like murdering her at the time I regretted having hit her long before I reached home. Twice I nearly turned back. Everything she had complained about was fair and I wondered if I dared phone her from home. Although Carla and I had only been lovers for a few months, she must have known how much I cared.

If Elizabeth had intended to comment on my

being late, she changed her mind the moment I handed her the roses. She began to arrange them in a vase while I poured myself a large whisky. I waited for her to say something as I rarely drank before dinner but she seemed preoccupied with the flowers. Although I had already made up my mind to phone Carla and try to make amends, I decided I couldn't do it from home. In any case, if I waited until the morning when I was back in the office, she might by then have calmed down a little.

I woke early the next day and lay in bed, considering what form my apology should take. I decided to invite her to lunch at the little French bistro she liked so much, half way between my office and hers. Carla always appreciated seeing me in the middle of the day, when she knew it couldn't be for sex. After I had shaved and dressed I joined Elizabeth for breakfast, and seeing there was nothing interesting on the front page, I turned to the financial section. The company's shares had fallen again, following City forecasts of poor interim profits. Millions would undoubtedly be wiped off our share value following such a bad piece of publicity. I already knew that when it came to publishing the annual accounts it would be a miracle if the company didn't declare a loss.

After gulping down a second cup of coffee I kissed my wife on the cheek and made for the car. It was then that I decided to drop a note through Carla's letterbox rather than cope with the embarrassment of a phone call.

'Forgive me,' I wrote. 'Marcel's, one o'clock. *Sole Véronique* on a Friday. Love, Casaneva.' I rarely wrote to Carla, and when I did I only ever signed it with her chosen nickname.

I took a short detour so that I could pass her home but was held up by a traffic jam. As I approached the flat I could see that the hold-up was being caused by some sort of accident. It had to be quite a serious one because there was an ambulance blocking the other side of the road and delaying the flow of oncoming vehicles. A traffic warden was trying to help but she was only slowing things down even more. It was obvious that it was going to be impossible to park anywhere near Carla's flat, so I resigned myself to phoning her from the office. I did not relish the prospect.

I felt a sinking feeling moments later when I saw that the ambulance was parked only a few yards from the front door to her block of flats. I knew I was being irrational but I began to fear the worst. I tried to convince myself it was probably a road accident and had nothing to do with Carla.

It was then that I spotted the police car tucked in behind the ambulance.

As I drew level with the two vehicles I saw that Carla's front door was wide open. A man in a long white coat came scurrying out and opened the back of the ambulance. I stopped my car to observe more carefully what was going on, hoping the man behind me would not become impatient. Drivers coming from the other direction raised a hand to thank me for allowing them to pass. I thought I could let a dozen or so through before anyone would start to complain. The traffic warden helped by urging them on.

Then a stretcher appeared at the end of the hall. Two uniformed orderlies carried a shrouded body out on to the road and placed it in the back of the ambulance. I was unable to see the face because it was covered by the sheet, but a third man, who could only have been a detective, walked immediately behind the stretcher. He was carrying a plastic bag, inside which I could make out a red garment that I feared was the negligee I had given Carla.

I vomited my breakfast all over the passenger seat, my head finally resting on the steering wheel. A moment later they closed the ambulance door, a siren started up and the traffic warden began waving me on. The ambulance moved quickly off and the man behind me started to press his horn. He was, after all, only an innocent bysitter. I lurched forward and later couldn't recall any part of my journey to the office.

Once I had reached the office car park I cleared up the mess on the passenger seat as best I could and left a window open before taking a lift to the washroom on the seventh floor. I tore my lunch invitation to Carla into little pieces and flushed them down the lavatory. I walked into my room on the twelfth floor a little after eight thirty, to find the managing director pacing up and down in front of my desk, obviously waiting for me. I had quite forgotten that it was

Friday and he always expected the latest completed figures to be ready for his consideration.

This Friday it turned out he also wanted the projected accounts for the months of May, June and July. I promised they would be on his desk by midday. The one thing I needed was a clear morning and I was not going to be allowed it.

Every time the phone rang, the door opened or anyone even spoke to me, my heart missed a beat – I assumed it could only be the police. By midday I had finished some sort of report for the managing director, but I knew he would find it neither adequate nor accurate. As soon as I had deposited the papers with his secretary, I left for an early lunch. I realised I wouldn't be able to eat anything, but at least I could get hold of the first edition of the *Standard* and search for any news they might have picked up about Carla's death.

I sat in the corner of my local pub where I knew I couldn't be seen from behind the bar. A tomato juice by my side, I began slowly to turn the pages of the paper.

She hadn't made page one. She hadn't made the second, third or fourth page. And on page five she rated only a tiny paragraph. 'Miss Carla Moorland, aged 31, was found dead at her home in Pimlico earlier this morning.' I remember thinking at the time they hadn't even got her age right. 'Detective Inspector Simmons, who has been put in charge of the case, said that an investigation was being carried out and they were awaiting the pathologist's report but to date they had no reason to suspect foul play.'

After that piece of news I even managed a little soup and a roll. Once I had read the report a second time I made my way back to the office car park and sat in my car. I wound down the other front window to allow more fresh air in before turning on the *World At One* on the radio. Carla didn't even get a mention. In the age of pump shotguns, drugs, Aids and gold bullion robberies the death of a thirty-two-year-old industrial personal assistant had passed unnoticed by the BBC.

I returned to my office to find on my desk a memo containing a series of questions that had been fired back from the managing director, leaving me in no doubt as to how he felt about my report. I was able to deal with nearly all his queries and return the answers to his secretary before I left the office that night, despite spending most of the afternoon trying to convince myself that whatever had caused Carla's death must have happened after I left and could not possibly have been connected with my hitting her. But that red negligee kept returning to my thoughts. Was there any way they could trace it back to me? I had bought it at Harrods – an extravagance, but I felt certain it couldn't be unique and it was still the only serious present I'd ever given her. But the note that was attached – had Carla destroyed it? Would they discover who Casaneva was?

I drove directly home that evening, aware that I

would never again be able to travel down the road Carla had lived in. I listened to the end of the *PM* programme on my car radio and as soon as I reached home switched on the six o'clock news. I turned to Channel Four at seven and back to the BBC at nine. I returned to ITV at ten and even ended up watching *Newsnight.*

Carla's death, in their combined editorial opinion, must have been less important than a Third-Division football result between Reading and Walsall. Elizabeth continued reading her latest library book, oblivious to my possible peril.

I slept fitfully that night, and as soon as I heard the papers pushed through the letterbox the next morning I ran downstairs to check the headlines.

'DUKAKIS NOMINATED AS CANDIDATE' stared up at me from the front page of *The Times.*

I found myself wondering, irrelevantly, if he would ever be President. 'President Dukakis' didn't sound quite right to me.

I picked up my wife's *Daily Express* and the three-word headline filled the top of the page: 'LOVERS' TIFF MURDER'.

My legs gave way and I fell to my knees. I must have made a strange sight, crumpled up on the floor trying to read that opening paragraph. I couldn't make out the words of the second paragraph without my spectacles. I stumbled back upstairs with the papers and grabbed the glasses from the table on my side of the bed. Elizabeth was still sleeping soundly. Even so,

I locked myself in the bathroom where I could read the story slowly and without fear of interruption.

> Police are now treating as murder the death of a beautiful Pimlico secretary, Carla Moorland, 32, who was found dead in her flat early yesterday morning. Detective Inspector Simmons of Scotland Yard, who is in charge of the case, initially considered Carla Moorland's death to be due to natural causes, but an X-ray has revealed a broken jaw which could have been caused in a fight.
>
> An inquest will be held on April 19th.
>
> Miss Moorland's daily, Maria Lucia (48), said – exclusively to the *Express* – that her employer had been with a man friend when she had left the flat at five o'clock on the night in question. Another witness, Mrs Rita Johnson, who lives in the adjoining block of flats, stated she had seen a man leaving Miss Moorland's flat at around six, before entering the newsagents opposite and later driving away. Mrs Johnson added that she couldn't be sure of the make of the car but it might have been a Rover . . .

'Oh, my God,' I exclaimed in such a loud voice that I was afraid it might have woken Elizabeth. I shaved and showered quickly, trying to think as I went along. I was dressed and ready to leave for work even before my wife had woken. I kissed her on the cheek but she only turned over, so I scribbled a note and left it on her side of the bed, explaining that I had to spend the morning in the office as I had an important report to complete.

On my journey to work I rehearsed exactly what I was going to say. I went over it again and again. I arrived on the twelfth floor a little before eight and left my door wide open so I would be aware of the slightest intrusion. I felt confident that I had a clear fifteen, even twenty minutes before anyone else could be expected to arrive.

Once again I went over exactly what I needed to say. I found the number in the L–R directory and scribbled it down on a pad in front of me before writing five headings in block capitals, something I always did before a board meeting.

BUS STOP

COAT

NO. 19

BMW

TICKET

Then I dialled the number.

I took off my watch and placed it in front of me. I had read somewhere that the location of a telephone call can be traced in about three minutes.

A woman's voice said, 'Scotland Yard.'

'Inspector Simmons, please,' was all I volunteered.

'Can I tell him who's calling?'

'No, I would prefer not to give my name.'

'Yes, of course, sir,' she said, evidently used to such callers.

Another ringing tone. My mouth went dry as a man's voice announced 'Simmons' and I heard the detective speak for the first time. I was taken aback to find that a man with so English a name could have such a strong Glaswegian accent.

'Can I help you?' he asked.

'No, but I think I can help you,' I said in a quiet tone which I pitched considerably lower than my natural speaking voice.

'How can you help me, sir?'

'Are you the officer in charge of the Carla-what-ever-her-name-is case?'

'Yes, I am. But how can you help?' he repeated.

The second hand showed one minute had already passed.

'I saw a man leaving her flat that night.'

'Where were you at the time?'

'At the bus stop on the same side of the road.'

'Can you give me a description of the man?' Simmons's tone was every bit as casual as my own.

'Tall. I'd say five eleven, six foot. Well built. Wore one of those posh City coats – you know, the black ones with a velvet collar.'

'How can you be so sure about the coat?' the detective asked.

'It was so cold standing out there waiting for the No. 19 that I wished it had been me who was wearing it.'

'Do you remember anything in particular that happened after he left the flat?'

'Only that he went into the paper shop opposite before getting into his car and driving away.'

'Yes, we know that much,' said the Detective Inspector. 'I don't suppose you recall what make of car it was?'

Two minutes had now passed and I began to watch the second hand more closely.

'I think it was a BMW,' I said.

'Do you remember the colour by any chance?'

'No, it was too dark for that.' I paused. 'But I saw him tear a parking ticket off the windscreen, so it shouldn't be too hard for you to trace him.'

'And at what time did all this take place?'

'Around six fifteen to six thirty, Inspector,' I said.

'And can you tell me . . . ?'

Two minutes fifty-eight seconds. I put the phone back on the hook. My whole body broke out in a sweat.

'Good to see you in the office on a Saturday morning,' said the managing director grimly as he passed my door. 'Soon as you're finished whatever you're doing I'd like a word with you.'

I left my desk and followed him along the corridor into his office. For the next hour he went over my projected figures, but however hard I tried I couldn't concentrate. It wasn't long before he stopped trying to disguise his impatience.

'Have you got something else on your mind?' he asked as he closed his file. 'You seem preoccupied.'

'No,' I insisted, 'just been doing a lot of overtime lately,' and stood up to leave.

Once I had returned to my office, I burnt the piece of paper with the five headings and left to go home. In the first edition of the afternoon paper, the 'Lovers' Tiff' story had been moved back to page seven. They had nothing new to report.

The rest of Saturday seemed interminable but my wife's *Sunday Express* finally brought me some relief.

'Following up information received in the Carla Moorland "Lovers' Tiff" murder, a man is helping the police with their inquiries.' The commonplace expressions I had read so often in the past suddenly took on a real meaning.

I scoured the other Sunday papers, listened to every news bulletin and watched each news item on television. When my wife became curious I explained that there was a rumour in the office that the company might be taken over again, which meant I could lose my job.

By Monday morning the *Daily Express* had named the man in 'The Lovers' Tiff murder' as Paul Menzies (51), an insurance broker from Sutton. His wife was at a hospital in Epsom under sedation while he was being held in the cells of Brixton Prison under arrest. I began to wonder if Mr Menzies had told Carla the truth about his wife and what *his* nickname might be. I poured myself a strong black coffee and left for the office.

Later that morning, Menzies appeared before the magistrates at the Horseferry Road court, charged with the murder of Carla Moorland. The police had been successful in opposing bail, the *Standard* reassured me.

It takes six months, I was to discover, for a case of this gravity to reach the Old Bailey. Paul Menzies passed those months on remand in Brixton Prison. I spent the same period fearful of every telephone call, every knock on the door, every unexpected visitor. Each one created its own nightmare. Innocent people have no idea how many such incidents occur every day. I went about my job as best I could, often wondering if Menzies knew of my relationship with Carla, if he knew my name or if he even knew of my existence.

It must have been a couple of months before the trial was due to begin that the company held its annual general meeting. It had taken some considerable creative accountancy on my part to produce a set of figures that showed us managing any profit at all. We certainly didn't pay our shareholders a dividend that year.

I came away from the meeting relieved, almost elated. Six months had passed since Carla's death and not one incident had occurred during that period to suggest that anyone suspected I had even known her, let alone been the cause of her death. I still felt guilty about Carla, even missed her, but after six months I was now able to go for a whole day without fear entering my mind. Strangely, I felt no guilt about Menzies's plight. After all, it was he who had become the instrument that was going to keep me from a lifetime spent in prison. So when the blow came it had double the impact.

It was on August 26th – I shall never forget it – that I received a letter which made me realise it might be necessary to follow every word of the trial. However much I tried to convince myself I should explain why I couldn't do it, I knew I wouldn't be able to resist it.

That same morning, a Friday – I suppose these things always happen on a Friday – I was called in for what I assumed was to be a routine weekly meeting with the managing director, only to be informed that the company no longer needed me.

'Frankly, in the last few months your work has gone from bad to worse,' I was told.

I didn't feel able to disagree with him.

'And you have left me with no choice but to replace you.'

A polite way of saying, 'You're sacked.'

'Your desk will be cleared by five this evening,' the managing director continued, 'when you will receive a cheque from the accounts department for £17,500.'

I raised an eyebrow.

'Six months' compensation, as stipulated in your contract when we took over the company,' he explained.

When the managing director stretched out his hand it was not to wish me luck, but to ask for the keys of my Rover.

I remember my first thought when he informed me of his decision: at least I would be able to attend every day of the trial without any hassle.

Elizabeth took the news of my sacking badly but only asked what plans I had for finding a new job. During the next month I pretended to look for a position in another company but realised I couldn't hope to settle down to anything until the case was over.

On the morning of the trial all the popular papers had colourful background pieces. The *Daily Express* even displayed on its front page a flattering picture of Carla in a swimsuit on the beach at Marbella: I wondered how much her sister in Fulham had been paid for that particular item. Alongside it was a profile photo of Paul Menzies which made him look as if he were already a convict.

I was amongst the first to be told in which court at the Old Bailey the case of the Crown v. Menzies would be tried. A uniformed policeman gave me detailed directions and along with several others I made my way to Court No. 4.

Once I had reached the courtroom I filed in and made sure that I sat on the end of my row. I looked round thinking everyone would stare at me, but to my relief no one showed the slightest interest.

I had a good view of the defendant as he stood in the dock. Menzies was a frail man who looked as if he had recently lost a lot of weight; fifty-one, the newspapers had said, but he looked nearer seventy. I began to wonder how much I must have aged over the past few months.

Menzies wore a smart, dark blue suit that hung loosely on him, a clean shirt and what I thought must be a regimental tie. His grey thinning hair was swept straight back; a small silver moustache gave him a military air. He certainly didn't look like a murderer or much of a catch as a lover, but anyone glancing towards me would probably have come to the same conclusion. I searched around the sea of faces for Mrs Menzies but no one in the court fitted the newspaper description of her.

We all rose when Mr Justice Buchanan came in. 'The Crown v. Menzies,' the clerk of the court read out.

The judge leaned forward to tell Menzies that he could be seated and then turned slowly towards the jury box.

He explained that, although there had been considerable press interest in the case, their opinion was all that mattered because they alone would be asked to decide if the prisoner were guilty or not guilty of murder. He also advised the jury against reading any newspaper articles concerning the trial or listening to anyone else's views, especially those who had not been present in court: such people, he said, were always the first to have an immutable opinion on what the verdict should be. He went on to remind the jury how important it was to concentrate on the evidence because a man's life was at stake. I found myself nodding in agreement.

I glanced round the court hoping there was nobody there who would recognise me. Menzies's eyes remained fixed firmly on the judge, who was turning back to face the prosecuting counsel.

Even as Sir Humphrey Mountcliff rose from his place on the bench I was thankful he was against Menzies and not me. A man of dominating height with a high forehead and silver grey hair, he commanded the court not only with his physical presence but with a voice that was never less than authoritative.

To a silent assembly he spent the rest of the morning setting out the case for the prosecution. His eyes rarely left the jury box except occasionally to peer down at his notes.

He reconstructed the events as he imagined they had happened that evening in April.

The opening address lasted two and a half hours, shorter than I'd expected. The judge then suggested a break for lunch and asked us all to be back in our places by ten past two.

After lunch Sir Humphrey called his first witness, Detective Inspector Simmons. I was unable to look directly at the policeman while he presented his evidence. Each reply he gave was as if he were addressing me personally. I wondered if he suspected all along that there was another man. Simmons gave a highly professional account of himself as he described in detail how they had found the body and later traced Menzies through two witnesses and the damning parking ticket. By the time Sir Humphrey sat down few people in that court could have felt that Simmons had arrested the wrong man.

Menzies's defence counsel, who rose to cross-examine the Detective Inspector, could not have been in greater contrast to Sir Humphrey. Mr Robert Scott, QC, was short and stocky, with thick bushy eyebrows. He spoke slowly and without inflection. I was happy to observe that one member of the jury was having difficulty in staying awake.

For the next twenty minutes Scott took the Detective Inspector painstakingly back over his evidence but was unable to make Simmons retract anything substantial. As the Inspector stepped out of the witness box I felt confident enough to look him straight in the eye.

The next witness was a Home Office pathologist, Dr Anthony Mallins, who, after answering a few preliminary questions to establish his professional status, moved on to answer an inquiry from Sir Humphrey that took everyone by surprise. The pathologist informed the court that there was clear evidence to suggest that Miss Moorland had had sexual intercourse shortly before her death.

'How can you be so certain, Dr Mallins?'

'Because I found traces of blood group B on the deceased's upper thigh, while Miss Moorland was later found to be blood group O. There were also traces of seminal fluid on the negligee she was wearing at the time of her death.'

'Are these common blood groups?' Sir Humphrey asked.

'Blood group O is common,' Dr Mallins admitted. 'Group B, however, is fairly unusual.'

'And what would you say was the cause of her death?' Sir Humphrey asked.

'A blow or blows to the head, which caused a broken jaw, and lacerations at the base of the skull which may have been delivered by a blunt instrument.'

I wanted to stand up and say, 'I can tell you which!' when Sir Humphrey said, 'Thank you, Dr Mallins. No more questions. Please wait there.'

Mr Scott treated the doctor with far more respect than he had Inspector Simmons, despite Mallins being the defendant's witness.

'Could the blow on the back of Miss Moorland's head have been caused by a fall?' he asked.

The doctor hesitated. 'Possibly,' he agreed. 'But that wouldn't explain the broken jaw.'

Mr Scott ignored the comment and pressed on.

'What percentage of people in Britain are blood group B?'

'About five, six per cent,' volunteered the doctor.

'Two and a half million people,' said Mr Scott, and waited for the figure to sink in before he suddenly changed tack.

But as hard as he tried he could not shift the pathologist on the time of death or on the fact that sexual intercourse must have taken place around the hours his client had been with Carla.

When Mr Scott sat down the judge asked Sir Humphrey if he wished to re-examine.

'I do, my Lord. Dr Mallins, you told the court that Miss Moorland suffered from a broken jaw and lacerations on the back of her head. Could the lacerations have been caused by falling on to a blunt object after the jaw had been broken?'

'I must object, my Lord,' said Mr Scott, rising with unusual speed. 'This is a leading question.'

Mr Justice Buchanan leaned forward and peered down at the doctor. 'I agree, Mr Scott, but I would like to know if Dr Mallins found blood group O, Miss Moorland's blood group, on any other object in the room?'

'Yes, my Lord,' replied the doctor. 'On the edge of the glass table in the centre of the room.'

'Thank you, Dr Mallins,' said Sir Humphrey. 'No more questions.'

Sir Humphrey's next witness was Mrs Rita Johnson, the lady who claimed she had seen everything.

'Mrs Johnson, on the evening of April 7th, did you see a man leave the block of flats where Miss Moorland lived?' Sir Humphrey asked.

'Yes, I did.'

'At about what time was that?'

'A few minutes after six.'

'Please tell the court what happened next.'

'He walked across the road, removed a parking ticket, got into his car and drove away.'

'Do you see that man in the court today?'

'Yes,' she said firmly, pointing to Menzies, who at this suggestion shook his head vigorously.

'No more questions.'

Mr Scott rose slowly again.

'What did you say was the make of the car the man got into?'

'I can't be sure,' Mrs Johnson said, 'but I think it was a BMW.'

'Not a Rover as you first told the police the following morning?'

The witness did not reply.

'And did you actually see the man in question remove a parking ticket from the car windscreen?' Mr Scott asked.

'I think so, sir, but it all happened so quickly.'

'I'm sure it did,' said Mr Scott. 'In fact, I suggest to you that it happened so quickly that you've got the wrong man and the wrong car.'

'No, sir,' she replied, but without the same conviction with which she had delivered her earlier replies.

Sir Humphrey did not re-examine Mrs Johnson. I realised that he wanted her evidence to be forgotten by the jury as quickly as possible. As it was, when she left the witness box she also left everyone in court in considerable doubt.

Carla's daily, Maria Lucia, was far more convincing. She stated unequivocally that she had seen Menzies in the living room of the flat that afternoon when she arrived a little before five. However, she had, she admitted, never seen him before that day.

'But isn't it true,' asked Sir Humphrey, 'that you usually only work in the mornings?'

'Yes,' she replied. 'Although Miss Moorland was in the habit of bringing work home on a Thursday afternoon so it was convenient for me to come in and collect my wages.'

'And how was Miss Moorland dressed that afternoon?' asked Sir Humphrey.

'In her blue morning coat,' replied the daily.

'Is this how she usually dressed on a Thursday afternoon?'

'No, sir, but I assumed she was going to have a bath before going out that evening.'

'But when you left the flat was she still with Mr Menzies?'

'Yes, sir.'

'Do you remember anything else she was wearing that day?'

'Yes, sir. Underneath the morning coat she wore a red negligee.'

My negligee was duly produced and Maria Lucia identified it. At this point I stared directly at the witness but she showed not a flicker of recognition. I thanked all the gods in the Pantheon that I had never once been to visit Carla in the morning.

'Please wait there,' were Sir Humphrey's final words to Miss Lucia.

Mr Scott rose to cross-examine.

'Miss Lucia, you have told the court that the purpose of the visit was to collect your wages. How long were you at the flat on this occasion?'

'I did a little clearing up in the kitchen and ironed a blouse, perhaps twenty minutes.'

'Did you see Miss Moorland during this time?'

'Yes, I went into the drawing room to ask if she would like some more coffee but she said no.'

'Was Mr Menzies with her at the time?'

'Yes, he was.'

'Were you at any time aware of a quarrel between the two of them or even raised voices?'

'No, sir.'

'When you saw them together did Miss Moorland show any signs of distress or need of help?'

'No, sir.'

'Then what happened?'

'Miss Moorland joined me in the kitchen a few minutes later, gave me my wages and I let myself out.'

'When you were alone in the kitchen with Miss Moorland, did she give any sign of being afraid of her guest?'

'No, sir.'

'No more questions, my Lord.'

Sir Humphrey did not re-examine Maria Lucia

and informed the judge that he had completed the case for the prosecution. Mr Justice Buchanan nodded and said he felt that was enough for the day; but I wasn't convinced it was enough to convict Menzies.

When I got home that night Elizabeth did not ask me where I had been, and I did not volunteer any information. I spent the evening pretending to go over job applications.

The following morning I had a late breakfast and read the papers before returning to my place at the end of a row in Court No. 4, only a few moments before the judge made his entrance.

Mr Justice Buchanan, having sat down, adjusted his wig before calling on Mr Scott to open the case for the defence. Mr Scott, QC, was once again slow to rise – a man paid by the hour, I thought uncharitably. He started by promising the court that his opening address would be brief, and he then remained on his feet for the next two and a half hours.

He began the case for the defence by going over in detail the relevant parts, as he saw them, of Menzies's past. He assured us all that those who wished to dissect it later would only find an unblemished record. Paul Menzies was a happily married man who lived in Sutton with his wife and three children, Polly, aged twenty-one, Michael, nineteen, and Sally, sixteen. Two of the children were now at university and the youngest had just completed her GCSE.

Doctors had advised Mrs Menzies not to attend the trial, following her recent release from hospital. I noticed two of the women on the jury smile sympathetically.

Mr Menzies, Mr Scott continued, had been with the same firm of insurance brokers in the City of London for the past six years and, although he had not been promoted, he was a much respected member of the staff. He was a pillar of his local community, having served with the Territorial Army and on the committee of the local camera club. He had once even stood for the Sutton council. He could hardly be described as a serious candidate as a murderer.

Mr Scott then went on to the actual day of the killing and confirmed that Mr Menzies had an appointment with Miss Moorland on the afternoon in question, but in a strictly professional capacity with the sole purpose of helping her with a personal insurance plan. There could have been no other reason to visit Miss Moorland during office hours. He did not have sexual intercourse with her and he certainly did not murder her.

The defendant had left his client a few minutes after six. He understood she had intended to change before going out to dinner with her sister in Fulham. He had arranged to see her the following Wednesday at his office for the purpose of drawing up the completed policy. The defence, Mr Scott went on, would later produce a diary entry that would establish the truth of this statement.

The charge against the accused was, he submitted, based almost completely on circumstantial evidence. He felt confident that, when the trial reached its conclusion, the jury would be left with no choice but to release his client back into the bosom of his loving family. 'You must end this nightmare,' Mr Scott concluded. 'It has gone on far too long for an innocent man.'

At this point the judge suggested a break for lunch. During the meal I was unable to concentrate or even take in what was being said around me. The majority of those who had an opinion to give now seemed convinced that Menzies was innocent.

As soon as we returned, at ten past two, Mr Scott called his first witness: the defendant himself.

Paul Menzies left the dock and walked slowly over to the witness box. He took a copy of the New Testament in his right hand and haltingly read the words of the oath, from a card which he held in his left.

Every eye was fixed on him while Mr Scott began to guide his client carefully through the minefield of evidence.

Menzies became progressively more confident in his delivery as the day wore on, and when at four thirty the judge told the court, 'That's enough for today,' I was convinced that he would get off, even if only by a majority verdict.

I spent a fitful night before returning to my place on the third day fearing the worst. Would Menzies be released and would they then start looking for me?

Mr Scott opened the third morning as gently as he had begun the second, but he repeated so many questions from the previous day that it became obvious he was only steadying his client in preparation for prosecuting counsel. Before he finally sat down he asked Menzies for a third time, 'Did you ever have sexual intercourse with Miss Moorland?'

'No, sir. I had only met her for the first time that day,' Menzies replied firmly.

'And did you murder Miss Moorland?'

'Certainly not, sir,' said Menzies, his voice now strong and confident.

Mr Scott resumed his place, a look of quiet satisfaction on his face.

In fairness to Menzies, very little which takes place in normal life could have prepared anyone for cross-examination by Sir Humphrey Mountcliff. I could not have asked for a better advocate.

'I'd like to start, if I may, Mr Menzies,' he began, 'with what your counsel seems to set great store by as proof of your innocence.'

Menzies's thin lips remained in a firm straight line.

'The pertinent entry in your diary which suggests that you made a second appointment to see Miss Moorland, the murdered woman' – three words Sir Humphrey was to repeat again and again during his cross-examination – 'for the Wednesday after she had been killed.'

'Yes, sir,' said Menzies.

'This entry was made – correct me if I'm wrong –

following your Thursday meeting at Miss Moorland's flat.'

'Yes, sir,' said Menzies, obviously tutored not to add anything that might later help prosecuting counsel.

'So when did you make that entry?' Sir Humphrey asked.

'On the Friday morning.'

'After Miss Moorland had been killed?'

'Yes, but I didn't know.'

'Do you carry a diary on you, Mr Menzies?'

'Yes, but only a small pocket diary, not my large desk one.'

'Do you have it with you today?'

'I do.'

'May I be allowed to see it?'

Reluctantly Menzies took a small green diary out of his jacket pocket and handed it over to the clerk of the court, who in turn passed it on to Sir Humphrey. Sir Humphrey began to leaf through the pages.

'I see that there is no entry for your appointment with Miss Moorland for the afternoon on which she was murdered?'

'No, sir,' said Menzies. 'I put office appointments only in my desk diary, personal appointments are restricted to my pocket diary.'

'I understand,' said Sir Humphrey. He paused and looked up. 'But isn't it strange, Mr Menzies, that you agreed to an appointment with a client to discuss further business and you then trusted it to memory, when you so easily could have put it in the diary you carry around with you all the time before transferring it?'

'I might have written it down on a slip of paper at the time, but as I explained that's a personal diary.'

'Is it?' said Sir Humphrey as he flicked back a few more pages. 'Who is David Paterson?' he asked.

Menzies looked as if he were trying to place him.

'Mr David Paterson, 112 City Road, 11.30, January 9th this year,' Sir Humphrey read out to the court. Menzies looked anxious. 'We could subpoena Mr Paterson if you can't recall the meeting,' said Sir Humphrey helpfully.

'He's a client of my firm,' said Menzies in a quiet voice.

'A client of your firm,' Sir Humphrey repeated slowly. 'I wonder how many of those I could find if I went through your diary at a more leisurely pace?' Menzies bowed his head as Sir Humphrey passed the diary back to the clerk, having made his point.

'Now I should like to turn to some more important questions . . .'

'Not until after lunch, Sir Humphrey,' the judge intervened. 'It's nearly one and I think we'll take a break now.'

'As you wish, my Lord,' came back the courteous reply.

I left the court in a more optimistic mood, even though I couldn't wait to discover what could be more important than that diary. Sir Humphrey's emphasis on little lies, although they did not prove Menzies was a murderer, did show he was hiding something. I became anxious that during the break Mr Scott might advise Menzies to admit to his affair with Carla, and thus make the rest of his story appear more credible. To my relief, over the meal I learned that under English law Menzies could not consult his counsel while he was still in the witness box. I noticed when we returned to court that Mr Scott's smile had disappeared.

Sir Humphrey rose to continue his cross-examination.

'You have stated under oath, Mr Menzies, that you are a happily married man.'

'I am, sir,' said the defendant with feeling.

'Was your first marriage as happy, Mr Menzies?' asked Sir Humphrey casually. The defendant's cheeks drained of their colour. I quickly looked over towards Mr Scott who could not mask that this was information with which he had not been entrusted.

'Take your time before you answer,' said Sir Humphrey.

All eyes turned to the man in the witness box.

'No,' said Menzies and quickly added, 'but I was very young at the time. It was many years ago and all a ghastly mistake.'

'All a ghastly mistake?' repeated Sir Humphrey, looking straight at the jury. 'And how did that marriage end?'

'In divorce,' Menzies said quite simply.

'And what were the grounds for that divorce?'

'Cruelty,' said Menzies, 'but . . .'

'But . . . would you like me to read out to the jury what your first wife swore under oath in court that day?'

Menzies stood there shaking. He knew that 'No' would damn him and 'Yes' would hang him.

'Well, as you seem unable to advise us I will, with your permission, my Lord, read the statement made before Mr Justice Rodger on June 9th, 1961, at the Swindon County Court by the first Mrs Menzies.' Sir Humphrey cleared his throat. '"He used to hit me again and again, and it became so bad that I had to run away for fear he might one day kill me."' Sir Humphrey emphasised the last five words.

'She was exaggerating,' shouted Menzies from the witness box.

'How unfortunate that poor Miss Carla Moorland cannot be with us today to let us know if your story about her is also an exaggeration.'

'I object, my Lord,' said Mr Scott. 'Sir Humphrey is harassing the witness.'

'I agree,' said the judge. 'Tread more carefully in future, Sir Humphrey.'

'I apologise, my Lord,' said Sir Humphrey, sounding singularly unapologetic. He closed the file to which he had been referring and replaced it on the desk in front of him before taking up a new one. He opened it slowly, making sure all in the court were following every movement before he extracted a single sheet of paper.

'How many mistresses have you had since you were married to the second Mrs Menzies?'

'Objection, my Lord. How can this be relevant?'

'My Lord, it is relevant, I respectfully suggest. I intend to show that this was not a business relationship that Mr Menzies was conducting with Miss Moorland but a highly personal one.'

'The question can be put to the defendant,' ruled the judge.

Menzies said nothing as Sir Humphrey held up the sheet of paper in front of him and studied it.

'Take your time because I want the exact number,' Sir Humphrey said, looking over the top of his glasses.

The seconds ticked on as we all waited.

'Hm – three, I think,' Menzies said eventually in a voice that just carried. The gentlemen of the press began scribbling furiously.

'Three,' said Sir Humphrey, staring at his piece of paper in disbelief.

'Well, perhaps four.'

'And was the fourth Miss Carla Moorland?' Sir Humphrey asked. 'Because you had sexual intercourse with her that evening, didn't you?'

'No, I did not,' said Menzies, but by this time few in that courtroom could have believed him.

'Very well then,' continued Sir Humphrey, as he placed the piece of paper on the bench in front of him. 'But before I return to your relationship with Miss Moorland, let us discover the truth about the other four.'

I stared at the piece of paper from which Sir Humphrey had been reading. From where I was seated I could see that there was nothing written on it at all. A blank white sheet lay before him.

I was finding it hard to keep a grin off my face. Menzies's adulterous background was an unexpected bonus for me and the press – and I couldn't help wondering how Carla would have reacted if she had known about it.

Sir Humphrey spent the rest of the day making Menzies relate the details of his previous relationships with the four mistresses. The court was agog and the journalists continued to scribble away, knowing they were about to have a field day. When the court rose Mr Scott's eyes were closed.

I drove home that night feeling not a little pleased with myself; like a man who had just completed a good day's work.

On entering the courtroom the following morning I noticed people were beginning to acknowledge other regulars and nod. I found myself falling into the same pattern and greeted people silently as I took my regular position on the end of the bench.

Sir Humphrey spent the morning going over some of Menzies's other misdemeanours. We discovered that he had served in the Territorial Army for only five months and left after a misunderstanding with his commanding officer over how many hours he should have been spending on exercises during weekends and how much he had claimed in expenses for those hours. We also learned that his attempts to get on the local council sprung more from anger at being refused planning permission to build on a piece of land adjoining his house than from an altruistic desire to serve his fellow men. To be fair, Sir Humphrey could have made the Archangel Gabriel look like a soccer hooligan; but his trump card was still to come.

'Mr Menzies, I should now like to return to your version of what happened on the night Miss Moorland was killed.'

'Yes,' sighed Menzies in a tired voice.

'When you visit a client to discuss one of your policies, how long would you say such a consultation usually lasts?'

'Usually half an hour, an hour at the most,' said Menzies.

'And how long did the consultation with Miss Moorland take?'

'A good hour,' said Menzies.

'And you left her, if I remember your evidence correctly, a little after six o'clock.'

'That is correct.'

'And what time was your appointment?'

'At five o'clock, as was shown clearly in my desk diary,' said Menzies.

'Well, Mr Menzies, if you arrived at about five to keep your appointment with Miss Moorland and left a little after six, how did you manage to get a parking fine?'

'I didn't have any small change for the meter at the time,' said Menzies confidently. 'As I was already a couple of minutes late, I just risked it.'

'You just risked it,' repeated Sir Humphrey slowly. 'You are obviously a man who takes risks, Mr Menzies. I wonder if you would be good enough to look at the parking ticket in question.'

The clerk handed it up to Menzies.

'Would you read out to the court the hour and minute that the traffic warden has written in the little boxes to show when the offence occurred.'

Once again Menzies took a long time to reply.

'Four sixteen to four thirty,' he said eventually.

'I didn't hear that,' said the judge.

'Would you be kind enough to repeat what you said for the judge?' Sir Humphrey asked.

Menzies repeated the damning figures.

'So now we have established that you were in fact with Miss Moorland some time before four sixteen, and not, as I suggest you later wrote in your diary, five o'clock. That was just another lie, wasn't it?'

'No,' said Menzies. 'I must have arrived a little earlier than I realised.'

'At least an hour earlier, it seems. And I also suggest to you that you arrived at that early hour because your interest in Carla Moorland was not simply professional?'

'That's not true.'

'Then it wasn't your intention that she should become your mistress?'

Menzies hesitated long enough for Sir Humphrey to answer his own question. 'Because the business part of your meeting finished in the usual half hour, did it not, Mr Menzies?' He waited for a response but still none was forthcoming.

'What is your blood group, Mr Menzies?'

'I have no idea.'

Sir Humphrey without warning changed tack: 'Have you heard of DNA, by any chance?'

'No,' came back the puzzled reply.

'Deoxyribonucleic acid is a proven technique that shows genetic information can be unique to every individual. Blood or semen samples can be matched. Semen, Mr Menzies, is as unique as any fingerprint. With such a sample we would know immediately if you raped Miss Moorland.'

'I didn't rape her,' Menzies said indignantly.

'Nevertheless sexual intercourse did take place, didn't it?' said Sir Humphrey quietly.

Menzies remained silent.

'Shall I recall the Home Office pathologist and ask him to carry out a DNA test?'

Menzies still made no reply.

'And check your blood group?' Sir Humphrey paused. 'I will ask you once again, Mr Menzies. Did sexual intercourse between you and the murdered woman take place that Thursday afternoon?'

'Yes, sir,' said Menzies in a whisper.

'Yes, sir,' repeated Sir Humphrey so that the whole court could hear it.

'But it wasn't rape,' Menzies shouted back at Sir Humphrey.

'Wasn't it?' said Sir Humphrey.

'And I swear I didn't kill her.'

I must have been the only person in that court-room who knew he was telling the truth. All Sir Humphrey said was, 'No more questions, my Lord.'

Mr Scott tried manfully to resurrect his client's credibility during re-examination but the fact that Menzies had been caught lying about his relationship with Carla made everything he had said previously appear doubtful.

If only Menzies had told the truth about being Carla's lover, his story might well have been accepted. I wondered why he had gone through the charade – in order to protect his wife? Whatever the motive, it had only ended by making him appear guilty of a crime he hadn't committed.

I went home that night and ate the largest meal I had had for several days.

The following morning Mr Scott called two more witnesses. The first turned out to be the vicar of St Peter's, Sutton, who was there as a character witness to prove what a pillar of the community Menzies was. After Sir Humphrey had finished his cross-examination the vicar ended up looking like a rather kind, unworldly old man, whose knowledge of Menzies was based on the latter's occasional attendance at Sunday matins.

The second was Menzies's superior at the company they both worked for in the City. He was a far more impressive figure but he was unable to confirm that Miss Moorland had ever been a client of the company.

Mr Scott put up no more witnesses and informed Mr Justice Buchanan that he had completed the case for the defence. The judge nodded and, turning to Sir Humphrey, told him he would not be required to begin his final address until the following morning.

That heralded the signal for the court to rise.

Another long evening and an even longer night had to be endured by Menzies and myself. As on every other day during the trial, I made sure I was in my place the next morning before the judge entered.

Sir Humphrey's closing speech was masterful. Every little untruth was logged so that one began to accept that very little of Menzies's testimony could be relied on.

'We will never know for certain,' said Sir Humphrey, 'for what reason poor young Carla Moorland was murdered. Refusal to succumb to Menzies's advances? A fit of temper which ended with a blow that caused her to fall and later die alone? But there are, however, some things, members of the jury, of which we can be quite certain.

'We can be certain that Menzies was with the

murdered woman that day before the hour of four sixteen because of the evidence of the damning parking ticket.

'We can be certain that he left a little after six because we have a witness who saw him drive away, and he does not himself deny this evidence.

'And we can be certain that he wrote a false entry in his diary to make you believe he had a business appointment with the murdered woman at five, rather than a personal assignation some time before.

'And we can now be certain that he lied about having sexual intercourse with Miss Moorland a short time before she was killed, though we cannot be certain if intercourse took place before or after her jaw had been broken.' Sir Humphrey's eyes rested on the jury before he continued.

'We can, finally, establish, beyond reasonable doubt, from the pathologist's report, the time of death and that, therefore, Menzies was the last person who could possibly have seen Carla Moorland alive.

'Therefore no one else could have killed Carla Moorland – for do not forget Inspector Simmons's evidence – and if you accept that, you can be in no doubt that only Menzies could have been responsible for her death. And how damning you must have found it that he tried to hide the existence of a first wife who had left him on the grounds of his cruelty, and the four mistresses who left him we know not why or how. Only one less than Bluebeard,' Sir Humphrey added with feeling.

'For the sake of every young girl who lives on her own in our capital, you must carry out your duty, however painful that duty might be. And find Menzies guilty of murder.'

When Sir Humphrey sat down I wanted to applaud.

The judge sent us away for another break. Voices all around me were now damning Menzies. I listened contentedly without offering an opinion. I knew that if the jury convicted Menzies the file would be closed and no eyes would ever be turned in my direction. I was seated in my place before the judge appeared at ten past two. He called on Mr Scott.

Menzies's counsel put up a spirited defence of his client, pointing out that almost all the evidence that Sir Humphrey had come up with had been circumstantial, and that it was even possible someone else could have visited Carla Moorland after his client had left that night. Mr Scott's bushy eyebrows seemed almost to have a life of their own as he energetically emphasised that it was the prosecution's responsibility to prove their case beyond reasonable doubt and not his to disprove it, and that, in his opinion, his learned friend, Sir Humphrey, had failed to do so.

During his summing-up Scott avoided any mention of diary entries, parking tickets, past mistresses, sexual intercourse or questions of his client's role in the community. A latecomer listening only to the closing speeches might have been forgiven for thinking the two learned gentlemen were summarising different cases.

Mr Scott's expression became grim as he turned to face the jury for his summation. 'The twelve of you,' he said, 'hold the fate of my client in your hands. You must, therefore, be certain, I repeat, certain beyond reasonable doubt that Paul Menzies could have committed such an evil crime as murder.

'This is not a trial about Mr Menzies's lifestyle, his position in the community or even his sexual habits. If adultery were a crime I feel confident Mr Menzies would not be the only person in this courtroom to be in the dock today.' He paused as his eyes swept up and down the jury.

'For this reason I feel confident that you will find it in your hearts to release my client from the torment he has been put through during the last seven months. He has surely been shown to be an innocent man deserving of your compassion.'

Mr Scott sank down on the bench having, I felt, given his client a glimmer of hope.

The judge told us that he would not begin his own summing-up until Monday morning.

The weekend seemed interminable to me. By Monday I had convinced myself that enough members of the jury would feel there just had not been sufficient evidence to convict.

As soon as the trial was under way the judge began by explaining once again that it was the jury alone who must make the ultimate decision. It was not his job to let them know how he felt, but only to advise them on the law.

He went back over all the evidence, trying to put it in perspective, but he never gave as much as a hint as to his own opinions. When he had completed his summing-up late that afternoon he sent the jury away to consider their verdict.

I waited with nearly as much anxiety as Menzies must have done while I listened to others giving their opinion as the minutes ticked by in that little room. Then, four hours later, a note was sent up to the judge.

He immediately asked the jury to return to their places while the press flooded back into the courtroom, making it look like the House of Commons on Budget Day. The clerk dutifully handed up the note to Mr Justice Buchanan. He opened it and read what only twelve other people in the courtroom could have known.

He handed it back to the clerk who then read the note to a silent court.

Mr Justice Buchanan frowned before asking if there were any chance of a unanimous verdict being reached if he allowed more time. Once he had learned that it was proving impossible he reluctantly nodded his agreement to a majority verdict.

The jury disappeared downstairs again to continue their deliberations, and did not return to their places for another three hours. I could sense the tension in the court as neighbours sought to give opinions to each other in noisy whispers. The clerk called for silence as the judge waited for everyone to settle before he instructed the clerk to proceed.

When the clerk rose, I could hear the person next to me breathing.

'Would the Foreman please stand?'

I rose from my place.

'Have you reached a verdict on which at least ten of you are agreed?'

'We have, sir.'

'Do you find the defendant, Paul Menzies, guilty or not guilty?'

'Guilty,' I replied.

CLEAN SWEEP IGNATIUS

Few showed much interest when Ignatius Agarbi was appointed Nigeria's Minister of Finance. After all, the cynics pointed out, he was the seventeenth person to hold the office in seventeen years.

In Ignatius's first major policy statement to Parliament he promised to end graft and corruption in public life and warned the electorate that no one holding an official position could feel safe unless he led a blameless life. He ended his maiden speech with the words, 'I intend to clear out Nigeria's Augean stables.'

Such was the impact of the minister's speech that it failed to get a mention in the Lagos *Daily Times*. Perhaps the editor considered that, since the paper had covered the speeches of the previous sixteen ministers *in extenso*, his readers might feel they had heard it all before.

Ignatius, however, was not to be disheartened by the lack of confidence shown in him, and set about his new task with vigour and determination. Within days of his appointment he had caused a minor official at the Ministry of Trade to be jailed for falsifying documents relating to the import of grain. The next to feel the bristles of Ignatius's new broom was a leading Lebanese financier, who was deported without trial for breach of the exchange control regulations. A month later came an event which even Ignatius considered a personal coup: the arrest of the Inspector General of Police for accepting bribes – a perk the citizens of Lagos had in the past considered went with the job. When four months later the Police Chief was sentenced to eighteen months in jail, the new Finance Minister finally made the front page of the Lagos *Daily Times*. A leader on the centre page dubbed him 'Clean Sweep Ignatius', the new broom every guilty man feared. Ignatius's reputation as Mr Clean continued to grow as arrest followed arrest and unfounded rumours began circulating in the capital that even General Otobi, the Head of State, was under investigation by his own Finance Minister.

Ignatius alone now checked, vetted and authorised all foreign contracts worth over one hundred million dollars. And although every decision he made was meticulously scrutinised by his enemies, not a breath of scandal ever became associated with his name.

When Ignatius began his second year of office as Minister of Finance even the cynics began to acknowledge his achievements. It was about this time that General Otobi felt confident enough to call Ignatius in for an unscheduled consultation.

The Head of State welcomed the Minister to

Dodan Barracks and ushered him to a comfortable chair in his study overlooking the parade ground.

'Ignatius, I have just finished going over the latest budget report and I am alarmed by your conclusion that the Exchequer is still losing millions of dollars each year in bribes paid to go-betweens by foreign companies. Have you any idea into whose pockets this money is falling? That's what I want to know.'

Ignatius sat bolt upright, his eyes never leaving the Head of State.

'I suspect a great percentage of the money is ending up in private Swiss bank accounts but I am at present unable to prove it.'

'Then I will give you whatever added authority you require to do so,' said General Otobi. 'You can use any means you consider necessary to ferret out these villains. Start by investigating every member of my Cabinet, past and present. And show no fear or favour in your endeavours, no matter what their rank or connections.'

'For such a task to have any chance of success I would need a special letter of authority signed by you, General . . .'

'Then it will be on your desk by six o'clock this evening,' said the Head of State.

'And the rank of Ambassador Plenipotentiary whenever I travel abroad.'

'Granted.'

'Thank you,' said Ignatius, rising from his chair on the assumption that the audience was over.

'You may also need this,' said the General as they walked towards the door. The Head of State handed Ignatius a small automatic pistol. 'Because I suspect by now that you have almost as many enemies as I.'

Ignatius took the pistol from the soldier awkwardly, put it in his pocket and mumbled his thanks.

Without another word passing between the two men, Ignatius left his leader and was driven back to his Ministry.

Without the knowledge of the Governor of the Central Bank of Nigeria, and unhindered by any senior civil servants, Ignatius enthusiastically set about his new task. He researched alone at night, and by day discussed his findings with no one. Three months later he was ready to pounce.

The Minister selected the month of August to make an unscheduled visit abroad, as it was the time when most Nigerians went on holiday, and his absence would therefore not be worthy of comment.

He asked his Permanent Secretary to book him, his wife and their two children on a flight to Orlando, and to be certain that the tickets were charged to his personal account.

On their arrival in Florida, the family checked into the local Marriott Hotel. Ignatius then informed his wife, without warning or explanation, that he would be spending a few days in New York on business before rejoining them for the rest of the holiday. The following morning he left his family to the mysteries of Disney World while he took a flight to New York.

Clean Sweep Ignatius

It was a short taxi ride from LaGuardia to Kennedy, where, after a change of clothes and the purchase of a return tourist ticket for cash, he boarded a Swissair flight for Geneva unobserved.

Once he had arrived, Ignatius booked into an inconspicuous hotel, retired to bed and slept soundly for eight hours. Over breakfast the following morning he studied the list of banks he had so carefully drawn up after completing his research in Nigeria: each name was written out boldly in his own hand. Ignatius decided to start with Gerber et Cie whose building, he observed from the hotel bedroom, took up half the Avenue de Parchine. He checked the telephone number with the concierge before placing a call. The chairman agreed to see him at twelve o'clock.

Carrying only a battered briefcase, Ignatius arrived at the bank a few minutes before the appointed hour – an unusual occurrence for a Nigerian, thought the young man dressed in a smart grey suit, white shirt and grey silk tie, who was waiting in the marble hall to greet him. He bowed to the Minister, introducing himself as the chairman's personal assistant, and explained that he would accompany Ignatius to the chairman's office. The young executive led the Minister to a waiting lift and neither man uttered another word until they had reached the eleventh floor. A gentle tap on the chairman's door elicited '*Entrez*,' which the young man obeyed.

'The Nigerian Minister of Finance, sir.'

The chairman rose from behind his desk and

stepped forward to greet his guest. Ignatius could not help noticing that he too wore a grey suit, white shirt and grey silk tie.

'Good morning, Minister,' the chairman said. 'Won't you have a seat?' He ushered Ignatius towards a low glass table surrounded by comfortable chairs on the far side of the room. 'I have ordered coffee for both of us if that is acceptable.'

Ignatius nodded, placed the battered briefcase on the floor by the side of his chair and stared out of the large plate-glass window. He made some small-talk about the splendid view of the magnificent fountain while a girl served all three men with coffee.

Once the young woman had left the room Ignatius got down to business.

'My Head of State has requested that I visit your bank with a rather unusual request,' he began. Not a flicker of surprise appeared on the face of the chairman or his young assistant. 'He has honoured me with the task of discovering which Nigerian citizens hold numbered accounts with your bank.'

On learning this piece of information only the chairman's lips moved. 'I am not at liberty to disclose –'

'Allow me to put my case,' said the Minister, raising a white palm. 'First, let me assure you that I come with the absolute authority of my government.' Without another word, Ignatius extracted an envelope from his inside pocket with a flourish. He handed it to the chairman who removed the letter inside and read it slowly.

Once he had finished reading, the banker cleared his throat. 'This document, I fear, sir, carries no validity in my country.' He replaced it in the envelope and handed it back to Ignatius. 'I am, of course,' continued the chairman, 'not for one moment doubting that you have the full backing of your Head of State, both as a Minister and an Ambassador, but that does not change the bank's rule of confidentiality in such matters. There are no circumstances in which we would release the names of any of our account holders without their authority. I'm sorry to be of so little help, but those are, and will always remain, the bank rules.' The chairman rose to his feet, as he considered the meeting was now at an end; but he had not bargained for Clean Sweep Ignatius.

'My Head of State,' said Ignatius, softening his tone perceptibly, 'has authorised me to approach your bank to act as the intermediary for all future transactions between my country and Switzerland.'

'We are flattered by your confidence in us, Minister,' replied the chairman, who remained standing. 'However, I feel sure that you will understand that it cannot alter our attitude to our customers' confidentiality.'

Ignatius remained unperturbed.

'Then I am sorry to inform you, Mr Gerber, that our Ambassador in Geneva will be instructed to make an official communiqué to the Swiss Foreign Office about the lack of co-operation your bank has shown concerning requests for information about our nationals.' He waited for his words to sink in. 'You could avoid such embarrassment, of course, by simply letting me know the names of my countrymen who hold accounts with Gerber et Cie and the amounts involved. I can assure you we would not reveal the source of our information.'

'You are most welcome to lodge such a communiqué, sir, and I feel sure that our Minister will explain to your Ambassador in the most courteous of diplomatic language that the Foreign Ministry does not have the authority under Swiss law to demand such disclosures.'

'If that is the case, I shall instruct my own Ministry of Trade to halt all future dealings in Nigeria with any Swiss nationals until these names are revealed.'

'That is your privilege, Minister,' replied the chairman, unmoved.

'And we may also have to reconsider every contract currently being negotiated by your countrymen in Nigeria. And in addition I shall personally see to it that no penalty clauses are honoured.'

'Would you not consider such action a little precipitate?'

'Let me assure you, Mr Gerber, that I would not lose one moment of sleep over such a decision,' said Ignatius. 'Even if my efforts to discover those names were to bring your country to its knees I would not be moved.'

'So be it, Minister,' replied the chairman. 'However, it still does not alter the policy or the attitude of this bank to confidentiality.'

'If that remains the case, sir, this very day I shall give instructions to our Ambassador to close our Embassy in Geneva and I shall declare your Ambassador in Lagos *persona non grata.*'

For the first time the chairman raised his eyebrows.

'Furthermore,' continued Ignatius, 'I will hold a conference in London which will leave the world's press in no doubt of my Head of State's displeasure with the conduct of this bank. After such publicity I feel confident you will find that many of your customers would prefer to close their accounts, while others who have in the past considered you a safe haven may find it necessary to look elsewhere.'

The Minister waited but still the chairman did not respond.

'Then you leave me no choice,' said Ignatius, rising from his seat.

The chairman stretched out his arm, assuming that at last the Minister was leaving, only to watch with horror as Ignatius placed a hand in his jacket pocket and removed a small pistol. The two Swiss bankers froze as the Nigerian Minister of Finance stepped forward and pressed the muzzle against the chairman's temple.

'I need those names, Mr Gerber, and by now you must realise I will stop at nothing. If you don't supply them immediately I'm going to blow your brains out. Do you understand?'

The chairman gave a slight nod, beads of sweat appearing on his forehead. 'And he will be next,' said Ignatius, gesturing towards the young assistant, who stood speechless and paralysed a few paces away.

'Get me the names of every Nigerian who holds an account in this bank,' Ignatius said quietly, looking towards the young man, 'or I'll blow your chairman's brains all over his soft pile carpet. Immediately, do you hear me?' he added sharply.

The young man looked towards the chairman, who was now trembling but said quite clearly, *'Non, Pierre, jamais.'*

'D'accord,' replied the assistant in a whisper.

'You can't say I didn't give you every chance.' Ignatius pulled back the hammer. The sweat was now pouring down the chairman's face and the young man had to turn his eyes away as he waited in terror for the pistol shot.

'Excellent,' said Ignatius, as he removed the gun from the chairman's head and returned to his seat. Both bankers were still trembling and quite unable to speak.

The Minister picked up the battered briefcase by the side of his chair and placed it on the glass table in front of him. He pressed back the clasps and the lid flicked up.

The two bankers stared down at the neatly packed rows of hundred-dollar bills. Every inch of the briefcase had been taken up. The chairman quickly estimated that it probably amounted to around five million dollars.

'I wonder, sir,' said Ignatius, 'how I go about opening an account with your bank?'

A LA CARTE

ARTHUR HAPGOOD was demobbed on November 3rd, 1946. Within a month he was back at his old workplace on the shop-floor of the Triumph factory on the outskirts of Coventry.

The five years spent in the Sherwood Foresters, four of them as a quartermaster seconded to a tank regiment, only underlined Arthur's likely post-war fate, despite having hoped to find more rewarding work once the war was over. However, on returning to England he quickly discovered that in a 'land fit for heroes' jobs were not that easy to come by, and although he did not want to go back to the work he had done for five years before war had been declared, that of fitting wheels on cars, he reluctantly, after four weeks on the dole, went to see his former works' manager at Triumph.

'The job's yours if you want it, Arthur,' the works' manager assured him.

'And the future?'

'The car's no longer a toy for the eccentric rich or even just a necessity for the businessman,' the works' manager replied. 'In fact,' he continued, 'management are preparing for the "two-car family".'

'So they'll need even more wheels to be put on cars,' said Arthur forlornly.

'That's the ticket.'

Arthur signed on within the hour and it was only a matter of days before he was back into his old routine. After all, he often reminded his wife, it didn't take a degree in engineering to screw four knobs on to a wheel a hundred times a shift.

Arthur soon accepted the fact that he would have to settle for second best. However, second best was not what he planned for his son.

Mark had celebrated his fifth birthday before his father had even set eyes on him, but from the moment Arthur returned home he lavished everything he could on the boy.

Arthur was determined that Mark was not going to end up working on the shop-floor of a car factory for the rest of his life. He put in hours of overtime to earn enough money to ensure that the boy could have extra tuition in maths, general science and English. He felt well rewarded when the boy passed his eleven-plus and won a place at King Henry VIII Grammar School, and that pride did not falter when Mark went on to pass five O-levels and two years later added two A-levels.

Arthur tried not to show his disappointment when, on Mark's eighteenth birthday, the boy informed him that he did not want to go to university.

'What kind of career *are* you hoping to take up then, lad?' Arthur enquired.

'I've filled in an application form to join you on the shop-floor just as soon as I leave school.'

'But why would you –'

'Why not? Most of my friends who're leaving this term have already been accepted by Triumph, and they can't wait to get started.'

'You must be out of your mind.'

'Come off it, Dad. The pay's good and you've shown that there's always plenty of extra money to be picked up with overtime. And I don't mind hard work.'

'Do you think I spent all those years making sure you got a first-class education just to let you end up like me, putting wheels on cars for the rest of your life?' Arthur shouted.

'That's not the whole job and you know it, Dad.'

'You go there over my dead body,' said his father. 'I don't care what your friends end up doing, I only care about you. You could be a solicitor, an accountant, an army officer, even a schoolmaster. Why should you want to end up at a car factory?'

'It's better paid than schoolmastering for a start,' said Mark. 'My French master once told me that he wasn't as well off as you.'

'That's not the point, lad –'

'The point is, Dad, I can't be expected to spend the rest of my life doing a job I don't enjoy just to satisfy one of your fantasies.'

'Well, I'm not going to allow you to waste the rest

of your life,' said Arthur, getting up from the breakfast table. 'The first thing I'm going to do when I get in to work this morning is see that your application is turned down.'

'That isn't fair, Dad. I have the right to –'

But his father had already left the room, and did not utter another word to the boy before leaving for the factory.

For over a week father and son didn't speak to each other. It was Mark's mother who was left to come up with the compromise. Mark could apply for any job that met with his father's approval and as long as he completed a year at that job he could, if he still wanted to, reapply to work at the factory. His father for his part would not then put any obstacle in his son's way.

Arthur nodded. Mark also reluctantly agreed to the solution.

'But only if you complete the full year,' Arthur warned solemnly.

During those last days of the summer holiday Arthur came up with several suggestions for Mark to consider, but the boy showed no enthusiasm for any of them. Mark's mother became quite anxious that her son would end up with no job at all until, while helping her slice potatoes for dinner one night, Mark confided that he thought hotel management seemed the least unattractive proposition he had considered so far.

'At least you'd have a roof over your head and be regularly fed,' his mother said.

'Bet they don't cook as well as you, Mum,' said Mark as he placed the sliced potatoes on the top of the Lancashire hot-pot. 'Still, it's only a year.'

During the next month Mark attended several interviews at hotels around the country without success. It was then that his father discovered that his old company sergeant was head porter at the Savoy: immediately Arthur started to pull a few strings.

'If the boy's any good,' Arthur's old comrade-in-arms assured him over a pint, 'he could end up as a head porter, even a hotel manager.' Arthur seemed well satisfied, even though Mark was still assuring his friends that he would be joining them a year to the day.

On September 1st, 1959, Arthur and Mark Hapgood travelled together by bus to Coventry station. Arthur shook hands with the boy and promised him, 'Your mother and I will make sure it's a special Christmas this year when they give you your first leave. And don't worry – you'll be in good hands with "Sarge". He'll teach you a thing or two. Just remember to keep your nose clean.'

Mark said nothing and returned a thin smile as he boarded the train. 'You'll never regret it . . .' were the last words Mark heard his father say as the train pulled out of the station.

Mark regretted it from the moment he set foot in the hotel.

As a junior porter he started his day at six in the morning and ended at six in the evening. He was entitled to a fifteen-minute mid-morning break, a forty-five-minute lunch break and another fifteen-minute break around mid-afternoon. After the first month had passed he could not recall when he had been granted all three breaks on the same day, and he quickly learned that there was no one to whom he could protest. His duties consisted of carrying guests' cases up to their rooms, then lugging them back down again the moment they wanted to leave. With an average of three hundred people staying in the hotel each night the process was endless. The pay turned out to be half what his friends were getting back home and as he had to hand over all his tips to the head porter, however much overtime Mark put in, he never saw an extra penny. On the only occasion he dared to mention it to the head porter he was met with the words, 'Your time will come, lad.'

It did not worry Mark that his uniform didn't fit or that his room was six foot by six foot and overlooked Charing Cross Station, or even that he didn't get a share of the tips; but it did worry him that there was nothing he could do to please the head porter – however clean he kept his nose.

Sergeant Crann, who considered the Savoy nothing more than an extension of his old platoon, didn't have a lot of time for young men under his command who hadn't done their national service.

'But I wasn't *eligible* to do national service,' insisted Mark. 'No one born after 1939 was called up.'

'Don't make excuses, lad.'

'It's not an excuse, Sarge. It's the truth.'

'And don't call me "Sarge". I'm "Sergeant Crann" to you, and don't you forget it.'

'Yes, Sergeant Crann.'

At the end of each day Mark would return to his little box-room with its small bed, small chair and tiny chest of drawers, and collapse exhausted. The only picture in the room – of the Laughing Cavalier – was on the calendar that hung above Mark's bed. The date of September 1st, 1960, was circled in red to remind him when he would be allowed to re-join his friends at the factory back home. Each night before falling asleep he would cross out the offending day like a prisoner making scratch marks on a wall.

At Christmas Mark returned home for a four-day break, and when his mother saw the general state of the boy she tried to talk his father into allowing Mark to give up the job early, but Arthur remained implacable.

'We made an agreement. I can't be expected to get him a job at the factory if he isn't responsible enough to keep to his part of a bargain.'

During the holiday Mark waited for his friends outside the factory gate until their shift had ended and listened to their stories of weekends spent watching football, drinking at the pub and dancing to the Everly

Brothers. They all sympathised with his problem and looked forward to him joining them in September. 'It's only a few more months,' one of them reminded him cheerfully.

Far too quickly, Mark was on the journey back to London, where he continued unwillingly to hump cases up and down the hotel corridors for month after month.

Once the English rain had subsided the usual influx of American tourists began. Mark liked the Americans, who treated him as an equal and often tipped him a shilling when others would have given him only sixpence. But whatever the amount Mark received Sergeant Crann would still pocket it with the inevitable, 'Your time will come, lad.'

One such American for whom Mark ran around diligently every day during his fortnight's stay ended up presenting the boy with a ten-bob note as he left the front entrance of the hotel.

Mark said, 'Thank you, sir,' and turned round to see Sergeant Crann standing in his path.

'Hand it over,' said Crann as soon as the American visitor was well out of earshot.

'I was going to the moment I saw you,' said Mark, passing the note to his superior.

'Not thinking of pocketing what's rightfully mine, was you?'

'No, I wasn't,' said Mark. 'Though God knows I earned it.'

'Your time will come, lad,' said Sergeant Crann without much thought.

'Not while someone as mean as you is in charge,' replied Mark sharply.

'What was that you said?' asked the head porter, veering round.

'You heard me the first time, Sarge.'

The clip across the ear took Mark by surprise.

'You, lad, have just lost your job. Nobody, but nobody, talks to me like that.' Sergeant Crann turned and set off smartly in the direction of the manager's office.

The hotel manager, Gerald Drummond, listened to the head porter's version of events before asking Mark to report to his office immediately. 'You realise I have been left with no choice but to sack you,' were his first words once the door was closed.

Mark looked up at the tall, elegant man in his long, black coat, white collar and black tie. 'Am I allowed to tell you what actually happened, sir?' he asked.

Mr Drummond nodded, then listened without interruption as Mark gave his version of what had taken place that morning, and also disclosed the agreement he had entered into with his father. 'Please let me complete my final ten weeks,' Mark ended, 'or my father will only say I haven't kept my end of our bargain.'

'I haven't got another job vacant at the moment,'

protested the manager. 'Unless you're willing to peel potatoes for ten weeks.'

'Anything,' said Mark.

'Then report to the kitchen at six tomorrow morning. I'll tell the third chef to expect you. Only if you think the head porter is a martinet just wait until you meet Jacques, our *maître chef de cuisine*. He won't clip your ear, he'll cut it off.'

Mark didn't care. He felt confident that for just ten weeks he could face anything, and at five thirty the following morning he exchanged his dark blue uniform for a white top and blue and white check trousers before reporting for his new duties. To his surprise the kitchen took up almost the entire basement of the hotel, and was even more of a bustle than the lobby had been.

The third chef put him in the corner of the kitchen, next to a mountain of potatoes, a bowl of cold water and a sharp knife. Mark peeled through breakfast, lunch and dinner, and fell asleep on his bed that night without even enough energy left to cross a day off his calendar.

For the first week he never actually saw the fabled Jacques. With seventy people working in the kitchens Mark felt confident he could pass his whole period there without anyone being aware of him.

Each morning at six he would start peeling, then hand over the potatoes to a gangling youth called Terry who in turn would dice or cut them according to the third chef's instructions for the dish of the day.

Monday sauté, Tuesday mashed, Wednesday French-fried, Thursday sliced, Friday roast, Saturday croquette . . . Mark quickly worked out a routine which kept him well ahead of Terry and therefore out of any trouble.

Having watched Terry do his job for over a week Mark felt sure he could have shown the young apprentice how to lighten his workload quite simply, but he decided to keep his mouth closed: opening it might only get him into more trouble, and he was certain the manager wouldn't give him a second chance.

Mark soon discovered that Terry always fell badly behind on Tuesday's shepherd's pie and Thursday's Lancashire hot-pot. From time to time the third chef would come across to complain and he would glance over at Mark to be sure that it wasn't him who was holding the process up. Mark made certain that he always had a spare tub of peeled potatoes by his side so that he escaped censure.

It was on the first Thursday morning in August (Lancashire hot-pot) that Terry sliced off the top of his forefinger. Blood spurted all over the sliced potatoes and on to the wooden table as the lad began yelling hysterically.

'Get him out of here!' Mark heard the *maître chef de cuisine* bellow above the noise of the kitchen as he stormed towards them.

'And you,' he said, pointing at Mark, 'clean up mess and start slicing rest of potatoes. I 'ave eight hundred hungry customers still expecting to feed.'

'Me?' said Mark in disbelief. 'But –'

'Yes, you. You couldn't do worse job than idiot who calls himself trainee chef and cuts off finger.' The chef marched away, leaving Mark to move reluctantly across to the table where Terry had been working. He felt disinclined to argue while the calendar was there to remind him that he was down to his last twenty-five days.

Mark set about a task he had carried out for his mother many times. The clean, neat cuts were delivered with a skill Terry would never learn to master. By the end of the day, although exhausted, Mark did not feel quite as tired as he had in the past.

At eleven that night the *maître chef de cuisine* threw off his hat and barged out of the swing doors, a sign to everyone else they could also leave the kitchen once everything that was their responsibility had been cleared up. A few seconds later the door swung back open and the chef burst in. He stared round the kitchen as everyone waited to see what he would do next. Having found what he was looking for, he headed straight for Mark.

'Oh, my God,' thought Mark. 'He's going to kill me.'

'How is your name?' the chef demanded.

'Mark Hapgood, sir,' he managed to splutter out.

'You waste on 'tatoes, Mark Hapgood,' said the chef. 'You start on vegetables in morning. Report at seven. If that crétin with half finger ever returns, put him to peeling 'tatoes.'

The chef turned on his heel even before Mark had

the chance to reply. He dreaded the thought of having to spend three weeks in the middle of the kitchens, never once out of the *maître chef de cuisine*'s sight, but he accepted there was no alternative.

The next morning Mark arrived at six for fear of being late and spent an hour watching the fresh vegetables being unloaded from Covent Garden market. The hotel's supply manager checked every case carefully, rejecting several before he signed a chit to show the hotel had received over three thousand pounds' worth of vegetables. An average day, he assured Mark.

The *maître chef de cuisine* appeared a few minutes before seven thirty, checked the menus and told Mark to score the Brussels sprouts, trim the French beans and remove the coarse outer leaves of the cabbages.

'But I don't know how,' Mark replied honestly. He could feel the other trainees in the kitchen edging away from him.

'Then I teach you,' roared the chef. 'Perhaps only thing you learn is if hope to be good chef, you able to do everyone's job in kitchen, even 'tato peeler's.'

'But I'm hoping to be a . . .' Mark began and then thought better of it. The chef seemed not to have heard Mark as he took his place beside the new recruit. Everyone in the kitchen stared as the chef began to show Mark the basic skills of cutting, dicing and slicing.

'And remember other idiot's finger,' the chef said on completing the lesson and passing the razor-sharp knife back to Mark. 'Yours can be next.'

Mark started gingerly dicing the carrots, then the Brussels sprouts, removing the outer layer before cutting a firm cross in the stalk. Next he moved on to trimming and slicing the beans. Once again he found it fairly easy to keep ahead of the chef's requirements.

At the end of each day, after the head chef had left, Mark stayed on to sharpen all his knives in preparation for the following morning, and would not leave his work area until it was spotless.

On the sixth day, after a curt nod from the chef, Mark realised he must be doing something half-right. By the following Saturday he felt he had mastered the simple skills of vegetable preparation and found himself becoming fascinated by what the chef himself was up to. Although Jacques rarely addressed anyone as he marched round the acre of kitchen except to grunt his approval or disapproval – the latter more commonly – Mark quickly learned to anticipate his needs. Within a short space of time he began to feel that he was part of a team – even though he was only too aware of being the novice recruit.

On the deputy chef's day off the following week Mark was allowed to arrange the cooked vegetables in their bowls and spent some time making each dish look attractive as well as edible. The chef not only noticed but actually muttered his greatest accolade – '*Bon.*'

During his last three weeks at the Savoy Mark did not even look at the calendar above his bed.

One Thursday morning a message came down

from the under-manager that Mark was to report to his office as soon as was convenient. Mark had quite forgotten that it was August 31st – his last day. He cut ten lemons into quarters, then finished preparing the forty plates of thinly sliced smoked salmon that would complete the first course for a wedding lunch. He looked with pride at his efforts before folding up his apron and leaving to collect his papers and final wage packet.

'Where you think you're going?' asked the chef, looking up.

'I'm off,' said Mark. 'Back to Coventry.'

'See you Monday then. You deserve day off.'

'No, I'm going home for good,' said Mark.

The chef stopped checking the cuts of rare beef that would make up the second course of the wedding feast.

'Going?' he repeated as if he didn't understand the word.

'Yes. I've finished my year and now I'm off home to work.'

'I hope you found first-class hotel,' said the chef with genuine interest.

'I'm not going to work in a hotel.'

'A restaurant, perhaps?'

'No, I'm going to get a job at Triumph.'

The chef looked puzzled for a moment, unsure if it was his English or whether the boy was mocking him.

'What is – Triumph?'

'A place where they manufacture cars.'

'You will manufacture cars?'

'Not a whole car, but I will put the wheels on.'

'You put cars on wheels?' the chef said in disbelief.

'No,' laughed Mark. 'Wheels on cars.'

The chef still looked uncertain.

'So you will be cooking for the car workers?'

'No. As I explained, I'm going to put the wheels on the cars,' said Mark slowly, enunciating each word.

'That not possible.'

'Oh yes it is,' responded Mark. 'And I've waited a whole year to prove it.'

'If I offered you job as commis chef, you change mind?' asked the chef quietly.

'Why would you do that?'

'Because you 'ave talent in those fingers. In time I think you become chef, perhaps even good chef.'

'No, thanks. I'm off to Coventry to join my mates.'

The head chef shrugged. '*Tant pis*,' he said, and without a second glance returned to the carcass of beef. He glanced over at the plates of smoked salmon. 'A wasted talent,' he added after the swing door had closed behind his potential protégé.

Mark locked his room, threw the calendar in the wastepaper basket and returned to the hotel to hand in his kitchen clothes to the housekeeper. The final action he took was to return his room key to the under-manager.

'Your wage packet, your cards and your PAYE. Oh, and the chef has phoned up to say he would be happy to give you a reference,' said the under-manager. 'Can't pretend that happens every day.'

'Won't need that where I'm going,' said Mark. 'But thanks all the same.'

He started off for the station at a brisk pace, his small battered suitcase swinging by his side, only to find that each step took a little longer. When he arrived at Euston he made his way to Platform 7 and began walking up and down, occasionally staring at the great clock above the booking hall. He watched first one train and then another pull out of the station bound for Coventry. He was aware of the station becoming dark as shadows filtered through the glass awning on to the public concourse. Suddenly he turned and walked off at an even brisker pace. If he hurried he could still be back in time to help chef prepare dinner that night.

Mark trained under Jacques le Renneu for five years. Vegetables were followed by sauces, fish by poultry, meats by pâtisserie. After eight years at the Savoy he was appointed second chef, and had learned so much from his mentor that regular patrons could no longer be sure when it was the *maître chef de cuisine*'s day off. Two years later Mark became a master chef, and when in 1971 Jacques was offered the opportunity to return to Paris and take over the kitchens of the George Cinq – an establishment that is to Paris what Harrods is to London – Jacques agreed, but only on condition that Mark accompanied him.

'It is wrong direction from Coventry,' Jacques warned him, 'and in any case they sure to offer you my job at the Savoy.'

'I'd better come along otherwise those Frogs will never get a decent meal.'

'Those Frogs,' said Jacques, 'will always know when it's my day off.'

'Yes, and book in even greater numbers,' suggested Mark, laughing.

It was not to be long before Parisians were flocking to the George Cinq, not to rest their weary heads but to relish the cooking of the two-chef team.

When Jacques celebrated his sixty-fifth birthday the great hotel did not have to look far to appoint his successor.

'The first Englishman ever to be *maître chef de cuisine* at the George Cinq,' said Jacques, raising a glass of champagne at his farewell banquet. 'Who would believe it? Of course, you will have to change your name to Marc to hold down such a position.'

'Neither will ever happen,' said Mark.

'Oh yes it will, because I 'ave recommended you.'

'Then I shall turn it down.'

'Going to put cars on wheels, *peut-être?*' asked Jacques mockingly.

'No, but I have found a little restaurant on the Left Bank. With my savings alone I can't quite afford the lease, but with your help . . .'

Chez Jacques opened on the rue du Plaisir on the Left Bank on May 1st, 1982, and it was not long before those customers who had taken the George Cinq for granted transferred their allegiance.

Mark's reputation spread as the two chefs pioneered 'nouvelle cuisine', and soon the only way anyone could be guaranteed a table at the restaurant in under three weeks was to be a film star or a Cabinet Minister.

The day Michelin gave Chez Jacques their third star Mark, with Jacques's blessing, decided to open a second restaurant. The press and customers then quarrelled amongst themselves as to which was the finer establishment. The booking sheets showed clearly the public felt there was no difference.

When in October 1986 Jacques died, at the age of seventy-one, the restaurant critics wrote confidently that standards were bound to fall. A year later the same journalists had to admit that one of the five great chefs of France had come from a town in the British Midlands they could not even pronounce.

Jacques's death only made Mark yearn more for his homeland, and when he read in the *Daily Telegraph* of a new development to be built in Covent Garden he called the site agent to ask for more details.

Mark's third restaurant was opened in the heart of London on February 11th, 1987.

Over the years Mark Hapgood often travelled back to Coventry to see his parents. His father had retired long since but Mark was still unable to persuade either parent to take the trip to Paris and sample his culinary efforts. But now he had opened in the country's capital he hoped to tempt them.

'We don't need to go up to London,' said his mother, laying the table. 'You always cook for us whenever you come home, and we read of your successes in the papers. In any case, your father isn't so good on his legs nowadays.'

'What do you call this, son?' his father asked a few minutes later as noisette of lamb surrounded by baby carrots was placed in front of him.

'Nouvelle cuisine.'

'And people pay good money for it?'

Mark laughed and the following day prepared his father's favourite Lancashire hot-pot.

'Now that's a real meal,' said Arthur after his third helping. 'And I'll tell you something for nothing, lad. You cook it almost as well as your mother.'

A year later Michelin announced the restaurants throughout the world that had been awarded their coveted third star. *The Times* let its readers know on its front page that Chez Jacques was the first English restaurant ever to be so honoured.

To celebrate the award Mark's parents finally agreed to make the journey down to London, though not until Mark had sent a telegram saying he was reconsidering that job at British Leyland. He sent a car to fetch his parents and had them installed in a suite at the Savoy. That evening he reserved the most popular table at Chez Jacques in their name.

Vegetable soup followed by steak and kidney pie with a plate of bread and butter pudding to end on were not the table d'hôte that night, but they were served for the special guests on Table 17.

Under the influence of the finest wine, Arthur was soon chatting happily to anyone who would listen and couldn't resist reminding the head waiter that it was his son who owned the restaurant.

'Don't be silly, Arthur,' said his wife. 'He already knows that.'

'Nice couple, your parents,' the head waiter confided to his boss after he had served them with their coffee and supplied Arthur with a cigar. 'What did your old man do before he retired? Banker, lawyer, schoolmaster?'

'Oh no, nothing like that,' said Mark quietly. 'He spent the whole of his working life putting wheels on cars.'

'But why would he waste his time doing that?' asked the waiter incredulously.

'Because he wasn't lucky enough to have a father like mine,' Mark replied.

NOT THE REAL THING

GERALD HASKINS and Walter Ramsbottom had been eating cornflakes for over a year.

'I'll swap you my MC and DSO for your VC,' said Walter, on the way to school one morning.

'Never,' said Gerald. 'In any case, it takes ten packet tops to get a VC and you only need two for an MC or a DSO.'

Gerald went on collecting packet tops until he had every medal displayed on the back of the packet.

Walter never got the VC.

Angela Bradbury thought they were both silly.

'They're only replicas,' she continually reminded them, 'not the real thing, and *I* am only interested in the real thing,' she told them haughtily.

Neither Gerald nor Walter cared for Angela's opinion at the time, both boys still being more interested in medals than the views of the opposite sex.

Kellogg's offer of free medals ended on January 1st, 1950, just at the time when Gerald had managed to complete the set.

Walter gave up eating cornflakes.

Children of the Fifties were then given the opportunity to discover the world of Meccano. Meccano demanded eating even more cornflakes and within a year Gerald had collected a large enough set to build bridges, pontoons, cranes and even an office block.

Gerald's family nobly went on munching cornflakes, but when he told them he wanted to build a whole town – Kellogg's positively final offer – it took nearly all his friends in the fifth form at Hull Grammar School to assist him in consuming enough breakfast cereal to complete his ambition.

Walter Ramsbottom refused to be of assistance.

Angela Bradbury's help was never sought.

All three continued on their separate ways.

Two years later, when Gerald Haskins won a place at Durham University, no one was surprised that he chose to read engineering and listed as his main hobby collecting medals.

Walter Ramsbottom joined his father in the family jewellery business and started courting Angela Bradbury.

It was during the spring holiday in Gerald's second year at Durham that he came across Walter and Angela again. They were sitting in the same row at a Bach quintet concert in Hull Town Hall. Walter told him in the interval that they had just become engaged but had not yet settled on a date for the wedding.

Gerald hadn't seen Angela for over a year but this

time he did listen to her opinions, because like Walter he fell in love with her.

He replaced eating cornflakes with continually inviting Angela out to dinner in an effort to win her away from his old rival.

Gerald notched up another victory when Angela returned her engagement ring to Walter a few days before Christmas.

Walter spread it around that Gerald only wanted to marry Angela because her father was chairman of the Hull City Amenities Committee and he was hoping to get a job with the council after he'd taken his degree at Durham. When the invitations for the wedding were sent out, Walter was not on the guest list.

Mr and Mrs Haskins travelled to Multavia for their honeymoon, partly because they couldn't afford Nice and didn't want to go to Cleethorpes. In any case, the local travel agent was making a special offer for those considering a visit to the tiny kingdom that was sandwiched between Austria and Czechoslovakia.

When the newly married couple arrived at their hotel in Teske, the capital, they discovered why the terms had been so reasonable.

Multavia was, in 1959, going through an identity crisis as it attempted to adjust to yet another treaty drawn up by a Dutch lawyer in Geneva, written in French, but with the Russians and Americans in mind. However, thanks to King Alfons III, their shrewd and popular monarch, the kingdom continued to enjoy uninterrupted grants from the West and non-disruptive visits from the East.

The capital of Multavia, the Haskins were quickly to discover, had an average temperature of 92°F in June, no rainfall and the remains of a sewerage system that had been indiscriminately bombed by both sides between 1939 and 1944. Angela actually found herself holding her nose as she walked through the cobbled streets. The People's Hotel claimed to have forty-five rooms, but what the brochure did not point out was that only three of them had bathrooms and none of those had bath plugs. Then there was the food, or lack of it; for the first time in his life Gerald lost weight.

The honeymoon couple were also to discover that Multavia boasted no monuments, art galleries, theatres or opera houses worthy of the name and the outlying country was flatter and less interesting than the fens of Cambridgeshire. The kingdom had no coastline and the only river, the Plotz, flowed from Germany and on into Russia, thus ensuring that none of the locals trusted it.

By the end of their honeymoon the Haskins were only too pleased to find that Multavia did not boast a national airline. BOAC got them home safely, and that would have been the end of Gerald's experience of Multavia had it not been for those sewers – or the lack of them.

*

Once the Haskins had returned to Hull, Gerald took up his appointment as an assistant in the engineering department of the city council. His first job was as a third engineer with special responsibility for the city's sewerage. Most ambitious young men would have treated such an appointment as nothing more than a step on life's ladder. Gerald however did not. He quickly made contact with all the leading sewerage companies, their advisers as well as his opposite numbers throughout the county.

Two years later he was able to put in front of his father-in-law's committee a paper showing how the council could save a considerable amount of the rate-payers' money by redeveloping its sewerage system.

The committee were impressed and decided to carry out Mr Haskins's recommendation, and at the same time appointed him second engineer.

That was the first occasion Walter Ramsbottom stood for the council; he wasn't elected.

When, three years later, the network of little tunnels and waterways had been completed, Gerald's diligence was rewarded by his appointment as deputy borough engineer. In the same year his father-in-law became Mayor and Walter Ramsbottom became a councillor.

Councils up and down the country were now acknowledging Gerald as a man whose opinion should be sought if they had any anxieties about their sewerage system. This provoked an irreverent round of jokes at every Rotary Club dinner Gerald attended, but they nevertheless still hailed him as the leading authority in his field, or drain.

When in 1966 the Borough of Halifax considered putting out to tender the building of a new sewerage system they first consulted Gerald Haskins – Yorkshire being the one place on earth where a prophet is with honour in his own country.

After spending a day in Halifax with the town council's senior engineer and realising how much had to be spent on the new system, Gerald remarked to his wife, not for the first time, 'Where there's muck there's brass.' But it was Angela who was shrewd enough to work out just how much of that brass her husband could get hold of with the minimum of risk. During the next few days Gerald considered his wife's proposition and when he returned to Halifax the following week it was not to visit the council chambers but the Midland Bank. Gerald did not select the Midland by chance; the manager of the bank was also chairman of the planning committee on the Halifax borough council.

A deal that suited both sides was struck between the two Yorkshiremen, and with the bank's blessing Gerald resigned his position as deputy borough engineer and formed a private company. When he presented his tender, in competition with several large organisations from London, no one was surprised that Haskins of Hull was selected unanimously by the planning committee to carry out the job.

Three years later Halifax had a fine new sewerage

system and the Midland Bank was delighted to be holding Haskins of Hull's company account.

Over the next fifteen years Chester, Runcorn, Huddersfield, Darlington, Macclesfield and York were jointly and severally grateful for the services rendered to them by Gerald Haskins, of Haskins & Co plc.

Haskins & Co (International) plc then began contract work in Dubai, Lagos and Rio de Janeiro. In 1983 Gerald received the Queen's Award for Industry from a grateful government, and a year later he was made a Commander of the British Empire by a grateful monarch.

The investiture took place at Buckingham Palace in the same year as King Alfons III of Multavia died and was succeeded by his son King Alfons IV. The newly crowned King decided something had finally to be done about the drainage problems of Teske. It had been his father's dying wish that his people should not go on suffering those unseemly smells, and King Alfons IV did not intend to bequeath the problem to *his* son.

After much begging and borrowing from the West, and much visiting and talking with the East, the newly anointed monarch decided to invite tenders for a new sewerage system in the kingdom's capital.

The tender document supplying several pages of details and listing the problems facing any engineer who wished to tackle the problem arrived with a thud on most of the boardroom tables of the world's major engineering companies. Once the paperwork had been seriously scrutinised and the realistic opportunity for a profit considered, King Alfons IV received only a few replies. Nevertheless, the King was able to sit up all night considering the merits of the three interested companies that had been short-listed. Kings are also human, and when Alfons discovered that Gerald had chosen Multavia for his honeymoon some twenty-five years before it tipped the balance. By the time Alfons IV fell asleep that morning he had decided to accept Haskins & Co (International) plc's tender.

And thus Gerald Haskins made his second visit to Multavia, this time accompanied by a site manager, three draughtsmen and eleven engineers. Gerald had a private audience with the King and assured him the job would be completed on time and for the price specified. He also told the King how much he was enjoying his second visit to his country. However, when he returned to England he assured his wife that there was still little in Multavia that could be described as entertainment before or after the hour of seven.

A few years later and after some considerable haggling over the increase in the cost of materials, Teske ended up with one of the finest sewerage systems in Central Europe. The King was delighted – although he continued to grumble about how Haskins & Co had over-run the original contract price. The words 'contingency payment' had to be explained to the monarch several times, who realised that the extra two hundred and forty thousand pounds would in turn have to be explained to the East and 'borrowed' from the West. After many veiled threats and 'without prejudice' solicitors' letters, Haskins & Co received the final payment but not until the King had been given a further grant from the British government, a payment which involved the Midland Bank, Sloane Street, transferring a sum of money to the Midland Bank, High Street, Hull, without Multavia ever getting their hands on it. This was after all, Gerald explained to his wife, how most overseas aid was distributed.

Thus the story of Gerald Haskins and the drainage problems of Teske might have ended, had not the British Foreign Secretary decided to pay a visit to the kingdom of Multavia.

The original purpose of the Foreign Secretary's European trip was to take in Warsaw and Prague, in order to see how *glasnost* and *perestroika* were working in those countries. But when the Foreign Office discovered how much aid had been allocated to Multavia and after they explained to their minister its role as a buffer state, the Foreign Secretary decided to accept King Alfons's long-standing invitation to visit the tiny kingdom. Such excursions to smaller countries by British Foreign Secretaries usually take place in airport lounges, a habit the British picked up from

Henry Kissinger, and later Comrade Gorbachev; but not on this occasion. It was felt Multavia warranted a full day.

As the hotels had improved only slightly since the time of Gerald's honeymoon, the Foreign Secretary was invited to lodge at the palace. He was asked by the King to undertake only two official engagements during his brief stay: the opening of the capital's new sewerage system, and a formal banquet.

Once the Foreign Secretary had agreed to these requests the King invited Gerald and his wife to be present at the opening ceremony – at their own expense. When the day of the opening came the Foreign Secretary delivered the appropriate speech for the occasion. He first praised Gerald Haskins on a remarkable piece of work in the great tradition of British engineering, then commended Multavia for her shrewd common sense in awarding the contract to a British company in the first place. The Foreign Secretary omitted to mention the fact that the British government had ended up underwriting the entire project. Gerald, however, was touched by the minister's words and said as much to the Foreign Secretary after the latter had pulled the lever that opened the first sluice gate.

That evening in the palace there was a banquet for over three hundred guests, including the ambassadorial corps and several leading British businessmen. There followed the usual interminable speeches about 'historic links', Multavia's role in Anglo-Soviet affairs and the 'special relationship' with Britain's own royal family.

The highlight of the evening, however, came after the speeches when the King made two investitures. The first was the award of the Order of the Peacock (Second Class) to the Foreign Secretary. 'The highest award a commoner can receive,' the King explained to the assembled audience, 'as the Order of the Peacock (First Class) is reserved for royalty and heads of state.'

The King then announced a second investiture. The Order of the Peacock (Third Class) was to be awarded to Gerald Haskins, CBE, for his work on the drainage system of Teske. Gerald was surprised and delighted as he was conducted from his place on the top table to join the King, who leaned forward to put a large gold chain encrusted with gems of various colours and sizes over his visitor's head. Gerald took two respectful paces backwards and bowed low, as the Foreign Secretary looked up from his seat and smiled encouragingly at him.

Gerald was the last foreign guest to leave the banquet that night. Angela, who had left on her own over two hours before, had already fallen asleep by the time Gerald returned to their hotel room. He placed the chain on the bed, undressed, put on his pyjamas, checked his wife was still asleep and then placed the chain back over his head to rest on his shoulders.

Gerald stood and looked at himself in the bathroom

mirror for several minutes. He could not wait to return home.

The moment Gerald got back to Hull he dictated a letter to the Foreign Office. He requested permission to be allowed to wear his new award on those occasions when it stipulated on the bottom right-hand corner of invitation cards that decorations and medals should be worn. The Foreign Office duly referred the matter to the Palace where the Queen, a distant cousin of King Alfons IV, agreed to the request.

The next official occasion at which Gerald was given the opportunity to sport the Order of the Peacock was the Mayor-making ceremony held in the chamber of Hull's City Hall, which was to be preceded by dinner at the Guildhall.

Gerald returned especially from Lagos for the occasion and even before changing into his dinner jacket couldn't resist a glance at the Order of the Peacock (Third Class). He opened the box that held his prize possession and stared down in disbelief: the gold had become tarnished and one of the stones looked as if it were coming loose. Mrs Haskins stopped dressing in order to steal a glance at the order. 'It's not gold,' she declared with a simplicity that would have stopped the IMF in their tracks.

Gerald offered no comment and quickly fixed the loose stone back in place with Araldite but he had to admit to himself that the craftmanship didn't bear careful scrutiny. Neither of them mentioned the subject again on their journey to Hull's City Hall.

Some of the guests during the Mayor's dinner that night at the Guildhall enquired after the history of the Order of the Peacock (Third Class), and although it gave Gerald some considerable satisfaction to explain how he had come by the distinction and indeed the Queen's permission to wear it on official occasions, he felt one or two of his colleagues had been less than awed by the tarnished peacock. Gerald also considered it was somewhat unfortunate that they had ended up on the same table as Walter Ramsbottom, now the Deputy Mayor.

'I suppose it would be hard to put a true value on it,' said Walter, staring disdainfully at the chain.

'It certainly would,' said Gerald firmly.

'I didn't mean a monetary value,' said the jeweller with a smirk. 'That would be only too easy to ascertain. I meant a sentimental value, of course.'

'Of course,' said Gerald. 'And are you expecting to be the Mayor next year?' he asked, trying to change the subject.

'It is the tradition,' said Walter, 'that the Deputy succeeds the Mayor if he doesn't do a second year. And be assured, Gerald, that I shall see to it that you are placed on the top table for that occasion.' Walter paused. 'The Mayor's chain, you know, is fourteen-carat gold.'

Gerald left the banquet early that evening determined to do something about the Order of the Peacock before it was Walter's turn to be Mayor.

None of Gerald's friends would have described

him as an extravagant man and even his wife was surprised at the whim of vanity that was to follow. At nine o'clock the next morning Gerald rang his office to say he would not be in to work that day. He then travelled by train to London to visit Bond Street in general and a famed jeweller in particular.

The door of the Bond Street shop was opened for Gerald by a sergeant from the Corps of Commissionaires. Once he had stepped inside Gerald explained his problem to the tall, thin gentleman in a black suit who had come forward to welcome him. He was then led to a circular glass counter in the middle of the shop floor.

'Our Mr Pullinger will be with you in a moment,' he was assured. Moments later Asprey's fine-gems expert arrived and happily agreed to Gerald's request to value the Order of the Peacock (Third Class). Mr Pullinger placed the chain on a black velvet cushion before closely studying the stones through a small eye glass.

After a cursory glance he frowned with the disappointment of a man who has won third prize at a shooting range on Blackpool pier.

'So what's it worth?' asked Gerald bluntly after several minutes had elapsed.

'Hard to put a value on something so intricately' – Pullinger hesitated – 'unusual.'

'The stones are glass and the gold's brass, that's what you're trying to say, isn't it, lad?'

Mr Pullinger gave a look that indicated that he could not have put it more succinctly himself.

'You might possibly be able to get a few hundred pounds from someone who collects such objects, but . . .'

'Oh, no,' said Gerald, quite offended. 'I have no interest in selling it. My purpose in coming up to London was to find out if you can *copy* it.'

'Copy it?' said the expert in disbelief.

'Aye,' said Gerald. 'First, I want every stone to be the correct gem according to its colour. Second, I expect a setting that would impress a duchess. And third, I require the finest craftsman put to work on it in nothing less than eighteen-carat gold.'

The expert from Asprey's, despite years of dealing with Arab clients, was unable to conceal his surprise.

'It would not be cheap,' he uttered *sotto voce*: the word 'cheap' was one of which Asprey's clearly disapproved.

'I never doubted that for one moment,' said Gerald. 'But you must understand that this is a once-in-a-lifetime honour for me. Now when could I hope to have an estimate?'

'A month, six weeks at the most,' replied the expert.

Gerald left the plush carpet of Asprey's for the sewers of Nigeria. When a little over a month later he flew back to London, he travelled in to the West End for his second meeting with Mr Pullinger.

The jeweller had not forgotten Gerald Haskins and his strange request, and he quickly produced from his order book a neatly folded piece of paper. Gerald unfolded it and read the tender slowly. Requirement for customer's request: twelve diamonds, seven amethysts, three rubies and a sapphire, all to be of the most perfect colour and of the highest quality. A peacock to be sculpted in ivory and painted by a craftsman. The entire chain then to be moulded in the finest eighteen-carat gold. The bottom line read: 'Two hundred and eleven thousand pounds – exclusive of VAT.'

Gerald, who would have thought nothing of haggling over an estimate of a few thousand pounds for roofing material or the hire of heavy equipment, or even a schedule of payments, simply asked, 'When will I be able to collect it?'

'One could not be certain how long it might take to put together such a fine piece,' said Mr Pullinger. 'Finding stones of a perfect match and colour will, I fear, take a little time.' He paused. 'I am also hoping that our senior craftsman will be free to work on this particular commission. He has been rather taken up lately with gifts for the Queen's forthcoming visit to Saudi Arabia so I don't think it could be ready before the end of March.'

Well in time for next year's Mayor's banquet, thought Gerald. Councillor Ramsbottom would not be able to mock him this time. Fourteen-carat gold, had he said?

Lagos and Rio de Janeiro both had their sewers down and running long before Gerald was able to return to Asprey's. And he only set his eyes on the unique prize a few weeks before Mayor-making day.

When Mr Pullinger first showed his client the finished work the Yorkshireman gasped with delight. The Order was so magnificent that Gerald found it necessary to purchase a string of pearls from Asprey's to ensure a silent wife.

On his return to Hull he waited until after dinner to open the green leather box from Asprey's and surprise her with the new Order. 'Fit for a monarch, lass,' he assured his wife but Angela seemed preoccupied with her pearls.

After Angela had left to wash up, her husband continued to stare for some time at the beautiful jewels so expertly crafted and superbly cut before he finally closed the box. The next morning he reluctantly took the piece round to the bank and explained that it must be kept safely locked in the vaults as he would only be requiring to take it out once, perhaps twice, a year. He couldn't resist showing the object of his delight to the bank manager, Mr Sedgley.

'You'll be wearing it for Mayor-making day, no doubt?' Mr Sedgley enquired.

'If I'm invited,' said Gerald.

'Oh, I feel sure Ramsbottom will want all his old friends to witness the ceremony. Especially you, I suspect,' he added without explanation.

Gerald read the news item in the Court Circular of *The Times* to his wife over breakfast: 'It has been announced from Buckingham Palace that King Alfons IV of Multavia will make a state visit to Britain between April 7th and 11th.'

'I wonder if we will have an opportunity to meet the King again,' said Angela.

Gerald offered no opinion.

In fact Mr and Mrs Gerald Haskins received two invitations connected with King Alfons's official visit, one to dine with the King at Claridge's – Multavia's London Embassy not being large enough to cater for such an occasion – and the second arriving a day later by special delivery from Buckingham Palace.

Gerald was delighted. The Peacock, it seemed, was going to get three outings in one month, as their visit to the Palace was ten days before Walter Ramsbottom would be installed as Mayor.

The state dinner at Claridge's was memorable and although there were several hundred other guests Gerald still managed to catch a moment with his host, King Alfons IV who, he found to his pleasure, could not take his eyes off the Order of the Peacock (Third Class).

The trip to Buckingham Palace a week later was Gerald and Angela's second, following Gerald's investiture in 1984 as a Commander of the British Empire. It took Gerald almost as long to dress for the state occasion as it did his wife. He took some time fiddling with his collar to be sure that his CBE could be seen to its full advantage while the Order of the Peacock still rested squarely on his shoulders. Gerald had asked his tailor to sew little loops into his tailcoat so that the Order did not have to be continually readjusted.

When the Haskins arrived at Buckingham Palace they followed a throng of bemedalled men and tiara'd ladies through to the state dining room where a footman handed out seating cards to each of the guests. Gerald unfolded his to find an arrow pointing to his name. He took his wife by the arm and guided her to their places.

He noticed that Angela's head kept turning whenever she saw a tiara.

Although they were seated some distance away from Her Majesty at an offshoot of the main table, there was still a minor royal on Gerald's left and the Minister of Agriculture on his right. He was more than satisfied. In fact the whole evening went far too quickly, and Gerald was already beginning to feel that Mayor-making day would be something of an anticlimax. Nevertheless, Gerald imagined a scene where Councillor Ramsbottom was admiring the Order of the Peacock (Third Class), while he was telling him about the dinner at the Palace.

After two loyal toasts and two national anthems the Queen rose to her feet. She spoke warmly of Multavia as she addressed her three hundred guests, and affectionately of her distant cousin the King. Her Majesty added that she hoped to visit his kingdom at some time in the near future. This was greeted with considerable applause. She then concluded her speech by saying it was her intention to make two investitures.

The Queen created King Alfons IV a Knight Commander of the Royal Victorian Order (KCVO), and then Multavia's Ambassador to the Court of St James a Commander of the same order (CVO), both being personal orders of the monarch. A box of royal blue was opened by the Court Chamberlain and the awards placed over the recipients' shoulders. As soon as the Queen had completed her formal duties, King Alfons rose to make his reply.

'Your Majesty,' he continued after the usual formalities and thanks had been completed. 'I also would like to make two awards. The first is to an Englishman who has given great service to my country through his expertise and diligence' – the King then glanced in Gerald's direction – 'a man,' he continued, 'who completed a feat of sanitary engineering that any nation on earth could be proud of and indeed, Your Majesty, it was opened by your own Foreign Secretary. We in the capital of Teske will remain in his debt for generations to come. We therefore bestow on

Mr Gerald Haskins, CBE, the Order of the Peacock (Second Class).'

Gerald couldn't believe his ears.

Tumultuous applause greeted a surprised Gerald as he made his way up towards their Majesties. He came to a standstill behind the throned chairs somewhere between the Queen of England and the King of Multavia. The King smiled at the new recipient of the Order of the Peacock (Second Class) as the two men shook hands. But before bestowing the new honour upon him, King Alfons leaned forward and with some difficulty removed from Gerald's shoulders his Order of the Peacock (Third Class).

'You won't be needing this any longer,' the King whispered in Gerald's ear.

Gerald watched in horror as his prize possession disappeared into a red leather box held open by the King's private secretary, who stood poised behind his sovereign. Gerald continued to stare at the private secretary, who was either a diplomat of the highest order or had not been privy to the King's plan, for his face showed no sign of anything untoward. Once Gerald's magnificent prize had been safely removed, the box snapped closed like a safe of which Gerald had not been told the combination.

Gerald wanted to protest, but remained speechless.

King Alfons then removed from another box the Order of the Peacock (Second Class) and placed it over Gerald's shoulders. Gerald, staring at the indifferent coloured glass stones, hesitated for a few moments before stumbling a pace back, bowing, and then returning to his place in the great dining room. He did not hear the waves of applause that accompanied him; his only thought was how he could possibly retrieve his lost chain immediately the speeches were over. He slumped down in the chair next to his wife.

'And now,' continued the King, 'I wish to present a decoration that has not been bestowed on anyone since my late father's death. The Order of the Peacock (First Class), which it gives me special delight to bestow on Her Majesty Queen Elizabeth II.'

The Queen rose from her place as the King's private secretary once again stepped forward. In his hands was held the same red leather case that had snapped shut so firmly on Gerald's unique possession. The case was re-opened and the King removed the magnificent Order from the box and placed it on the shoulders of the Queen. The jewels sparkled in the candlelight and the guests gasped at the sheer magnificence of the piece.

Gerald was the only person in the room who knew its true value.

'Well, you always said it was fit for a monarch,' his wife remarked as she touched her string of pearls.

'Aye,' said Gerald. 'But what's Ramsbottom going to say when he sees this?' he added sadly, fingering the Order of the Peacock (Second Class). 'He'll know it's not the real thing.'

'I don't see it matters that much,' said Angela.

'What do you mean, lass?' asked Gerald. 'I'll be the laughing stock of Hull on Mayor-making day.'

'You should start reading the evening papers, Gerald, and stop looking in mirrors and then you'd know Walter isn't going to be Mayor this year.'

'Not going to be Mayor?' repeated Gerald.

'No. The present Mayor has opted to do a second term so Walter won't be Mayor until next year.'

'Is that right?' said Gerald with a smile.

'And if you're thinking what I think you're thinking, Gerald Haskins, this time it's going to cost you a tiara.'

JUST GOOD FRIENDS

I woke up before him feeling slightly randy but I knew there was nothing I could do about it.

I blinked and my eyes immediately accustomed themselves to the half light. I raised my head and gazed at the large expanse of motionless white flesh lying next to me. If only he took as much exercise as I did he wouldn't have that spare tyre, I thought unsympathetically.

Roger stirred restlessly and even turned over to face me, but I knew he would not be fully awake until the alarm on his side of the bed started ringing. I pondered for a moment whether I could go back to sleep again or should get up and find myself some breakfast before he woke. In the end I settled for just lying still on my side day-dreaming, but making sure I didn't disturb him. When he did eventually open his eyes I planned to pretend I was still asleep – that way he would end up getting breakfast for me. I began to go over the things that needed to be done after he had left for the office. As long as I was at home ready to greet him when he returned from work, he didn't seem to mind what I got up to during the day.

A gentle rumble emanated from his side of the bed. Roger's snoring never disturbed me. My affection for him was unbounded, and I only wished I could find the words to let him know. In truth, he was the first man I had really appreciated. As I gazed at his unshaven face I was reminded that it hadn't been his looks which had attracted me in the pub that night.

I had first come across Roger in the Cat and Whistle, a public house situated on the corner of Mafeking Road. You might say it was our local. He used to come in around eight, order a pint of mild and take it to a small table in the corner of the room just beyond the dartboard. Mostly he would sit alone, watching the darts being thrown towards double top but more often settling in one or five, if they managed to land on the board at all. He never played the game himself, and I often wondered, from my vantage point behind the bar, if he were fearful of relinquishing his favourite seat or just had no interest in the sport.

Then things suddenly changed for Roger – for the better, was no doubt how he saw it – when one evening in early spring a blonde named Madeleine, wearing an imitation fur coat and drinking double gin and its, perched on the stool beside him. I had never seen her in the pub before but she was obviously known locally, and loose bar talk led me to believe it couldn't last. You see, word was about that she was looking for someone whose horizons stretched beyond the Cat and Whistle.

In fact the affair – if that's what it ever came to –

lasted for only twenty days. I know because I counted every one of them. Then one night voices were raised and heads turned as she left the small stool just as suddenly as she had come. His tired eyes watched her walk to a vacant place at the corner of the bar, but he didn't show any surprise at her departure and made no attempt to pursue her.

Her exit was my cue to enter. I almost leapt from behind the bar and, moving as quickly as dignity allowed, was seconds later sitting on the vacant stool beside him. He didn't comment and certainly made no attempt to offer me a drink, but the one glance he shot in my direction did not suggest he found me an unacceptable replacement. I looked around to see if anyone else had plans to usurp my position. The men standing round the dartboard didn't seem to care. Treble seventeen, twelve and a five kept them more than occupied. I glanced towards the bar to check if the boss had noticed my absence, but he was busy taking orders. I saw Madeleine was already sipping a glass of champagne from the pub's only bottle, purchased by a stranger whose stylish double-breasted blazer and striped bow tie convinced me she wouldn't be bothering with Roger any longer. She looked well set for at least another twenty days.

I looked up at Roger – I had known his name for some time, although I had never addressed him as such and I couldn't be sure that he was aware of mine. I began to flutter my eyelashes in a rather exaggerated way. I felt a little stupid but at least it elicited a gentle smile. He leaned over and touched my cheek, his hands surprisingly gentle. Neither of us felt the need to speak. We were both lonely and it seemed unnecessary to explain why. We sat in silence, he occasionally sipping his beer, I from time to time rearranging my legs, while a few feet from us the darts pursued their undetermined course.

When the publican cried, 'Last orders,' Roger downed the remains of his beer while the dart players completed what had to be their final game.

No one commented when we left together and I was surprised that Roger made no protest as I accompanied him back to his little semi-detached. I already knew exactly where he lived because I had seen him on several occasions standing at the bus queue in Dobson Street in a silent line of reluctant morning passengers. Once I even positioned myself on a nearby wall in order to study his features more carefully. It was an anonymous, almost commonplace face but he had the warmest eyes and the kindest smile I had observed in any man.

My only anxiety was that he didn't seem aware of my existence, just constantly preoccupied, his eyes each evening and his thoughts each morning only for Madeleine. How I envied that girl. She had everything I wanted – except a decent fur coat, the only thing my mother had left me. In truth, I have no right to be catty about Madeleine, as her past couldn't have been more murky than mine.

All that had taken place well over a year ago and,

to prove my total devotion to Roger, I have never entered the Cat and Whistle since. He seemed to have forgotten Madeleine because he never once spoke of her in front of me. An unusual man, he didn't question me about any of my past relationships either.

Perhaps he should have. I would have liked him to know the truth about my life before we'd met, though it all seems irrelevant now. You see, I had been the youngest in a family of four so I always came last in line. I had never known my father, and I arrived home one night to discover that my mother had run off with another man. Tracy, one of my sisters, warned me not to expect her back. She turned out to be right, for I have never seen my mother since that day. It's awful to have to admit, if only to oneself, that one's mother is a tramp.

Now an orphan, I began to drift, often trying to stay one step ahead of the law – not so easy when you haven't always got somewhere to put your head down. I can't even recall how I ended up with Derek – if that was his real name. Derek, whose dark sensual looks would have attracted any susceptible female, told me that he had been on a merchant steamer for the past three years. When he made love to me I was ready to believe anything. I explained to him that all I wanted was a warm home, regular food and perhaps in time a family of my own. He ensured that one of my wishes was fulfilled, because a few weeks after he left me I ended up with twins, two girls. Derek never set eyes on them: he had returned to sea even before

I could tell him I was pregnant. He hadn't needed to promise me the earth; he was so good-looking he must have known I would have been his just for a night on the tiles.

I tried to bring up the girls decently, but the authorities caught up with me this time and I lost them both. I wonder where they are now? God knows. I only hope they've ended up in a good home. At least they inherited Derek's irresistible looks, which can only help them through life. It's just one more thing Roger will never know about. His unquestioning trust only makes me feel more guilty, and now I never seem able to find a way of letting him know the truth.

After Derek had gone back to sea I was on my own for almost a year before getting part-time work at the Cat and Whistle. The publican was so mean that he wouldn't have even provided food and drink for me, if I hadn't kept to my part of the bargain.

Roger used to come in about once, perhaps twice a week before he met the blonde with the shabby fur coat. After that it was every night until she upped and left him.

I knew he was perfect for me the first time I heard him order a pint of mild. A pint of mild – I can't think of a better description of Roger. In those early days the barmaids used to flirt openly with him, but he didn't show any interest. Until Madeleine latched on to him I wasn't even sure that it was women he preferred. Perhaps in the end it was my androgynous looks that appealed to him.

I think I must have been the only one in that pub who was looking for something more permanent.

And so Roger allowed me to spend the night with him. I remember that he slipped into the bathroom to undress while I rested on what I assumed would be my side of the bed. Since that night he has never once asked me to leave, let alone tried to kick me out. It's an easy-going relationship. I've never known him raise his voice or scold me unfairly. Forgive the cliché, but for once I have fallen on my feet.

Brr. Brr. Brr. That damned alarm. I wished I could have buried it. The noise would go on and on until at last Roger decided to stir himself. I once tried to stretch across him and put a stop to its infernal ringing, only ending up knocking the contraption on to the floor, which annoyed him even more than the ringing. Never again, I concluded. Eventually a long arm emerged from under the blanket and a palm dropped on to the top of the clock and the awful din subsided. I'm a light sleeper – the slightest movement stirs me. If only he had asked me I could have woken him far more gently each morning. After all, my methods are every bit as reliable as any man-made contraption.

Half awake, Roger gave me a brief cuddle before kneading my back, always guaranteed to elicit a smile. Then he yawned, stretched and declared as he did every morning, 'Must hurry along or I'll be late for the office.' I suppose some females would have been annoyed by the predictability of our morning routine

– but not this lady. It was all part of a life that made me feel secure in the belief that at last I had found something worthwhile.

Roger managed to get his feet into the wrong slippers – always a fifty-fifty chance – before lumbering towards the bathroom. He emerged fifteen minutes later, as he always did, looking only slightly better than he had when he entered. I've learned to live with what some would have called his foibles, while he has learned to accept my mania for cleanliness and a need to feel secure.

'Get up, lazy-bones,' he remonstrated but then only smiled when I re-settled myself, refusing to leave the warm hollow that had been left by his body.

'I suppose you expect me to get your breakfast before I go to work?' he added as he made his way downstairs. I didn't bother to reply. I knew that in a few moments' time he would be opening the front door, picking up the morning newspaper, any mail, and our regular pint of milk. Reliable as ever, he would put on the kettle, then head for the pantry, fill a bowl with my favourite breakfast food and add my portion of the milk, leaving himself just enough for two cups of coffee.

I could anticipate almost to the second when breakfast would be ready. First I would hear the kettle boil, a few moments later the milk would be poured, then finally there would be the sound of a chair being pulled up. That was the signal I needed to confirm it was time for me to join him.

I stretched my legs slowly, noticing my nails needed some attention. I had already decided against a proper wash until after he had left for the office. I could hear the sound of the chair being scraped along the kitchen lino. I felt so happy that I literally jumped off the bed before making my way towards the open door. A few seconds later I was downstairs. Although he had already taken his first mouthful of cornflakes he stopped eating the moment he saw me.

'Good of you to join me,' he said, a grin spreading over his face.

I padded over towards him and looked up expectantly. He bent down and pushed my bowl towards me. I began to lap up the milk happily, my tail swishing from side to side.

It's a myth that we only swish our tails when we're angry.

THE STEAL

CHRISTOPHER AND MARGARET Roberts always spent their summer holiday as far away from England as they could possibly afford. However, as Christopher was the classics master at St Cuthbert's, a small preparatory school just north of Yeovil, and Margaret was the school matron, their experience of four of the five continents was largely confined to periodicals such as the *National Geographic Magazine* and *Time*.

The Roberts' annual holiday each August was nevertheless sacrosanct and they spent eleven months of the year saving, planning and preparing for their one extravagant luxury. The following eleven months were then spent passing on their discoveries to the 'offspring': the Roberts, without children of their own, looked on all the pupils of St Cuthbert's as 'offspring'.

During the long evenings when the 'offspring' were meant to be asleep in their dormitories, the Roberts would pore over maps, analyse expert opinion and then finally come up with a shortlist to consider. In recent expeditions they had been as far afield as Norway, Northern Italy and Yugoslavia, ending up the previous year exploring Achilles' island, Skyros, off the east coast of Greece.

'It has to be Turkey this year,' said Christopher after much soul-searching. A week later Margaret came to the same conclusion, and so they were able to move on to Phase Two. Every book on Turkey in the local library was borrowed, consulted, re-borrowed and re-consulted. Every brochure obtainable from the Turkish Embassy or local travel agents received the same relentless scrutiny.

By the first day of the summer term, charter tickets had been paid for, a car hired, accommodation booked and everything that could be insured comprehensively covered. Their plans lacked only one final detail.

'So what will be our "steal" this year?' asked Christopher.

'A carpet,' Margaret said, without hesitation. 'It has to be. For over a thousand years Turkey has produced the most sought-after carpets in the world. We'd be foolish to consider anything else.'

'How much shall we spend on it?'

'Five hundred pounds,' said Margaret, feeling very extravagant.

Having agreed, they once again swapped memories about the 'steals' they had made over the years. In Norway, it had been a whale's tooth carved in the shape of a galleon by a local artist who soon after had been taken up by Steuben. In Tuscany, it had been a ceramic bowl found in a small village where they cast and fired them to be sold in Rome at exorbitant prices: a small blemish which only an expert would have noticed made it a 'steal'. Just outside Skopje the Roberts had visited a local glass factory and acquired a water jug moments after it had been blown in front of their eyes, and in Skyros they had picked up their greatest triumph to date, a fragment of an urn they discovered near an old excavation site. The Roberts reported their find immediately to the authorities, but the Greek officials had not considered the fragment important enough to prevent it being exported to St Cuthbert's.

On returning to England Christopher couldn't resist just checking with the senior classics don at his old *alma mater*. He confirmed the piece was probably twelfth century. This latest 'steal' now stood, carefully mounted, on their drawing room mantelpiece.

'Yes, a carpet would be perfect,' Margaret mused. 'The trouble is, everyone goes to Turkey with the idea of picking up a carpet on the cheap. So to find a really good one. . . .'

She knelt and began to measure the small space in front of their drawing room fireplace.

'Seven by three should do it,' she said.

Within a few days of term ending, the Roberts travelled by bus to Heathrow. The journey took a little longer than by rail but at half the cost. 'Money saved is money that can be spent on the carpet,' Margaret reminded her husband.

'Agreed, Matron,' said Christopher, laughing.

On arrival at Heathrow they checked their baggage on to the charter flight, selected two non-smoking seats and, finding they had time to spare, decided to watch other planes taking off to even more exotic places.

It was Christopher who first spotted the two passengers dashing across the tarmac, obviously late.

'Look,' he said, pointing at the running couple. His wife studied the overweight pair, still brown from a previous holiday, as they lumbered up the steps to their plane.

'Mr and Mrs Kendall-Hume,' Margaret said in disbelief. After hesitating for a moment, she added, 'I wouldn't want to be uncharitable about any of the offspring, but I do find young Malcolm Kendall-Hume a . . .' She paused.

'"Spoilt little brat"?' suggested her husband.

'Quite,' said Margaret. 'I can't begin to think what his parents must be like.'

'Very successful, if the boy's stories are to be believed,' said Christopher. 'A string of second-hand garages from Birmingham to Bristol.'

'Thank God they're not on our flight.'

'Bermuda or the Bahamas would be my guess,' suggested Christopher.

A voice emanating from the loudspeaker gave Margaret no chance to offer her opinion.

'Olympic Airways Flight 172 to Istanbul is now boarding at Gate No. 37.'

'That's us,' said Christopher happily as they began their long route-march to their departure gate.

They were the first passengers to board, and once shown to their seats they settled down to study the guidebooks of Turkey and their three files of research.

'We must be sure to see Diana's Temple when we visit Ephesus,' said Christopher, as the plane taxied out on to the runway.

'Not forgetting that at that time we shall be only a few kilometres away from the purported last home of the Virgin Mary,' added Margaret.

'Taken with a pinch of salt by serious historians,' Christopher remarked as if addressing a member of the Lower Fourth, but his wife was too engrossed in her book to notice. They both continued to study on their own before Christopher asked what his wife was reading.

'*Carpets – Fact and Fiction* by Abdul Verizoglu – seventeenth edition,' she said, confident that any errors would have been eradicated in the previous sixteen. 'It's most informative. The finest examples, it seems, are from Hereke and are woven in silk and are sometimes worked on by up to twenty young women, even children, at a time.'

'Why young?' pondered Christopher. 'You'd have thought experience would have been essential for such a delicate task.'

'Apparently not,' said Margaret. 'Herekes are woven by those with young eyes which can discern intricate patterns sometimes no larger than a pinpoint and with up to nine hundred knots a square inch. Such a carpet,' continued Margaret, 'can cost as much as fifteen, even twenty, thousand pounds.'

'And at the other end of the scale? Carpets woven in old leftover wool by old leftover women?' suggested Christopher, answering his own question.

'No doubt,' said Margaret. 'But even for our humble purse there are some simple guidelines to follow.'

Christopher leaned over so that he could be sure to take in every word above the roar of the engines.

'The muted reds and blues with a green base are considered classic and are much admired by Turkish collectors, but one should avoid the bright yellows and oranges,' read his wife aloud. 'And never consider a carpet that displays animals, birds or fishes, as they are produced only to satisfy Western tastes.'

'Don't they like animals?'

'I don't think that's the point,' said Margaret. 'The Sunni Muslims, who are the country's religious rulers, don't approve of graven images. But if we search diligently round the bazaars we should still be able to come across a bargain for a few hundred pounds.'

'What a wonderful excuse to spend all day in the bazaars.'

Margaret smiled, before continuing. 'But listen. It's most important to bargain. The opening price the dealer offers is likely to be double what he expects to get and treble what the carpet is worth.' She looked up from her book. 'If there's any bargaining to be done it will have to be carried out by you, my dear. They're not used to that sort of thing at Marks & Spencer.'

Christopher smiled.

'And finally,' continued his wife, turning a page of her book, 'if the dealer offers you coffee you should accept. It means he expects the process to go on for some time as he enjoys the bargaining as much as the sale.'

'If that's the case they had better have a very large pot percolating for us,' said Christopher as he closed his eyes and began to contemplate the pleasures that awaited him. Margaret only closed her books on carpets when the plane touched down at Istanbul airport, and at once opened file Number One, entitled 'Pre-Turkey'.

'A shuttle bus should be waiting for us at the north side of the terminal. It will take us on to the local flight,' she assured her husband as she carefully wound her watch forward two hours.

The Roberts were soon following the stream of passengers heading in the direction of passport control. The first people they saw in front of them were the same middle-aged couple they had assumed were destined for more exotic shores.

'Wonder where they're heading,' said Christopher.

'Istanbul Hilton, I expect,' said Margaret as they climbed into a vehicle that had been declared redundant by the Glasgow Corporation Bus Company some twenty years before. It spluttered out black exhaust fumes as it revved up before heading off in the direction of the local THY flight.

The Roberts soon forgot all about Mr and Mrs Kendall-Hume once they looked out of the little aeroplane windows to admire the west coast of Turkey highlighted by the setting sun. The plane landed in the port of Izmir just as the shimmering red ball disappeared behind the highest hill. Another bus, even older than the earlier one, ensured that the Roberts reached their little guest house just in time for late supper.

Their room was tiny but clean and the owner much in the same mould. He greeted them both with exaggerated gesturing and a brilliant smile which augured well for the next twenty-one days. Early the following morning, the Roberts checked over their detailed plans for Day One in file Number Two. They were first to collect the rented Fiat that had already been paid for in England, before driving off into the hills to the ancient Byzantine fortress at Selcuk in the morning, to be followed by the Temple of Diana in the afternoon if they still had time.

After breakfast had been cleared away and they had cleaned their teeth, the Roberts left the guest house a few minutes before nine. Armed with their hire car form and guidebook, they headed off Tor Beyazik's Garage where their promised car awaited them. They strolled down the cobbled streets past the little white houses, enjoying the sea breeze until they reached the bay. Christopher spotted the sign for Beyazik's Garage when it was still a hundred yards ahead of them.

As they passed the magnificent yachts moored alongside the harbour, they tested each other on the nationality of each flag, feeling not unlike the 'off-spring' completing a geography test.

'Italian, French, Liberian, Panamanian, German. There aren't many British boats,' said Christopher, sounding unusually patriotic, the way he always did, Margaret reflected, the moment they were abroad.

She stared at the rows of gleaming hulls lined up like buses in Piccadilly during the rush hour; some of the boats were even bigger than buses. 'I wonder what kind of people can possibly afford such luxury?' she asked, not expecting a reply.

'Mr and Mrs Roberts, isn't it?' shouted a voice from behind them. They both turned to see a now-familiar figure dressed in a white shirt and white shorts, wearing a hat that made him look not unlike the 'Bird's Eye' captain, waving at them from the bow of one of the bigger yachts.

'Climb on board, me hearties,' Mr Kendall-Hume declared enthusiastically, more in the manner of a command than an invitation.

Reluctantly the Roberts walked the gangplank.

'Look who's here,' their host shouted down a large hole in the middle of the deck. A moment later Mrs Kendall-Hume appeared from below, dressed in a diaphanous orange sarong and a matching bikini top.

'It's Mr and Mrs Roberts – you remember, from Malcolm's school.'

Kendall-Hume turned back to face the dismayed couple. 'I don't remember your first names, but this is Melody and I'm Ray.'

'Christopher and Margaret,' the schoolmaster admitted as handshakes were exchanged.

'What about a drink? Gin, vodka or . . . ?'

'Oh, no,' said Margaret. 'Thank you very much, we'll both have an orange juice.'

'Suit yourselves,' said Ray Kendall-Hume. 'You must stay for lunch.'

'But we couldn't impose . . .'

'I insist,' said Mr Kendall-Hume. 'After all, we're on holiday. By the way, we'll be going over to the other side of the bay for lunch. There's one hell of a beach there, and it will give you a chance to sunbathe and swim in peace.'

'How considerate of you,' said Christopher.

'And where's young Malcolm?' asked Margaret.

'He's on a scouting holiday in Scotland. Doesn't like to mess about in boats the way we do.'

For the first time he could recall Christopher felt some admiration for the boy. A moment later the engine started thunderously.

On the trip across the bay, Ray Kendall-Hume expounded his theories about 'having to get away from it all'. 'Nothing like a yacht to ensure your privacy and not having to mix with the *hoi polloi*' He only wanted the simple things in life: the sun, the sea and an infinite supply of good food and drink.

The Roberts could have asked for nothing less. By the end of the day they were both suffering from a mild bout of sunstroke and were also feeling a little seasick. Despite white pills, red pills and yellow pills, liberally supplied by Melody, when they finally got back to their room that night they were unable to sleep.

Avoiding the Kendall-Humes over the next twenty days did not prove easy. Beyazik's, the garage where their little hire car awaited them each morning and to which it had to be returned each night, could only be reached via the quayside where the Kendall-Humes' motor yacht was moored like an insuperable barrier at a gymkhana. Hardly a day passed that the Roberts did not have to spend some part of their precious time bobbing up and down on Turkey's choppy coastal waters, eating oily food and discussing how large a carpet would be needed to fill the Kendall-Humes' front room.

However, they still managed to complete a large part of their programme and determinedly set aside the whole of the last day of the holiday in their quest for a carpet. As they did not need Beyazik's car to go into town, they felt confident that for that day at least they could safely avoid their tormentors.

On the final morning they rose a little later than

planned and after breakfast strolled down the tiny cobbled path together, Christopher in possession of the seventeenth edition of *Carpets – Fact and Fiction*, Margaret with a tape measure and five hundred pounds in travellers' cheques.

Once the schoolmaster and his wife had reached the bazaar they began to look around a myriad of little shops, wondering where they should begin their adventure. Fez-topped men tried to entice them to enter their tiny emporiums but the Roberts spent the first hour simply taking in the atmosphere.

'I'm ready to start the search now,' shouted Margaret above the babble of voices around her.

'Then we've found you just in time,' said the one voice they thought they had escaped.

'We were just about to –'

'Then follow me.'

The Roberts' hearts sank as they were led by Ray Kendall-Hume out of the bazaar and back towards the town.

'Take my advice, and you'll end up with one hell of a bargain,' Kendall-Hume assured them both. 'I've picked up some real beauties in my time from every corner of the globe at prices you wouldn't believe. I am happy to let you take full advantage of my expertise at no extra charge.'

'I don't know how you could stand the noise and smell of that bazaar,' said Melody, obviously glad to be back among the familiar signs of Gucci, Lacoste and Saint Laurent.

'We rather like . . .'

'Rescued in the nick of time,' said Ray Kendall-Hume. 'And the place I'm told you have to start and finish at if you want to purchase a serious carpet is Osman's.'

Margaret recalled the name from her carpet book: 'Only to be visited if money is no object and you know exactly what you are looking for.' The vital last morning was to be wasted, she reflected as she pushed open the large glass doors of Osman's to enter a ground-floor area the size of a tennis court. The room was covered in carpets on the floor, the walls, the windowsills, and even the tables. Anywhere a carpet could be laid out, a carpet was there to be seen. Although the Roberts realised immediately that nothing on show could possibly be in their price range, the sheer beauty of the display entranced them.

Margaret walked slowly round the room, mentally measuring the small carpets so she could anticipate the sort of thing they might look for once they had escaped.

A tall, elegant man, hands raised as if in prayer and dressed immaculately in a tailored worsted suit that could have been made in Savile Row, advanced to greet them.

'Good morning, sir,' he said to Mr Kendall-Hume, selecting the serious spender without difficulty. 'Can I be of assistance?'

'You certainly can,' replied Kendall-Hume. 'I want to be shown your finest carpets, but I do not intend to pay your finest prices.'

The dealer smiled politely and clapped his hands. Six small carpets were brought in by three assistants who rolled them out in the centre of the room. Margaret fell in love with a muted green-based carpet with a pattern of tiny red squares woven around the borders. The pattern was so intricate she could not take her eyes off it. She measured the carpet out of interest: seven by three exactly.

'You have excellent taste, madam,' said the dealer. Margaret, colouring slightly, quickly stood up, took a pace backwards and hid the tape measure behind her back.

'How do you feel about that lot, pet?' asked Kendall-Hume, sweeping a hand across the six carpets.

'None of them are big enough,' Melody replied, giving them only a fleeting glance.

The dealer clapped his hands a second time and the exhibits were rolled up and taken away. Four larger ones soon replaced them.

'Would you care for some coffee?' the dealer asked Mr Kendall-Hume as the new carpets lay unfurled at their feet.

'Haven't the time,' said Kendall-Hume shortly. 'Here to buy a carpet. If I want a coffee, I can always go to a coffee shop,' he said with a chuckle. Melody smiled her complicity.

'Well, I would like some coffee,' declared Margaret, determined to rebel at some point on the holiday.

'Delighted, madam,' said the dealer, and one of

the assistants disappeared to carry out her wishes while the Kendall-Humes studied the new carpets. The coffee arrived a few moments later. She thanked the young assistant and began to sip the thick black liquid slowly. Delicious, she thought, and smiled her acknowledgment to the dealer.

'Still not large enough,' Mrs Kendall-Hume insisted. The dealer gave a slight sigh and clapped his hands yet again. Once more the assistants began to roll up the rejected goods. He then addressed one of his staff in Turkish. The assistant looked doubtfully at his mentor but the dealer gave a firm nod and waved him away. The assistant returned a little later with a small platoon of lesser assistants carrying two carpets, both of which when unfolded took up most of the shop floor. Margaret liked them even less than the ones she had just been shown, but as her opinion was not sought she did not offer it.

'That's more like it,' said Ray Kendall-Hume. 'Just about the right size for the lounge, wouldn't you say, Melody?'

'Perfect,' his wife replied, making no attempt to measure either of the carpets.

'I'm glad we agree,' said Ray Kendall-Hume. 'But which one, my pet? The faded red and blue, or the bright yellow and orange?'

'The yellow and orange one,' said Melody without hesitation. 'I like the pattern of brightly coloured birds running round the outside.' Christopher thought he saw the dealer wince.

'So now all we have left to do is agree on a price,' said Kendall-Hume. 'You'd better sit down, pet, as this may take a while.'

'I hope not,' said Mrs Kendall-Hume, resolutely standing. The Roberts remained mute.

'Unfortunately, sir,' began the dealer, 'your wife has selected one of the finest carpets in our collection and so I fear there can be little room for any re-adjustment.'

'How much?' said Kendall-Hume.

'You see, sir, this carpet was woven in Demirdji, in the province of Izmir, by over a hundred seam-stresses and it took them more than a year to complete.'

'Don't give me that baloney,' said Kendall-Hume, winking at Christopher. 'Just tell me how much I'm expected to pay.'

'I feel it my duty to point out, sir, that this carpet shouldn't be here at all,' said the Turk plaintively. 'It was originally made for an Arab prince who failed to complete the transaction when the price of oil collapsed.'

'But he must have agreed on a price at the time?'

'I cannot reveal the exact figure, sir. It embarrasses me to mention it.'

'It wouldn't embarrass me,' said Kendall-Hume. 'Come on, what's the price?' he insisted.

'Which currency would you prefer to trade in?' the Turk asked.

'Pounds.'

The dealer removed a slim calculator from his jacket pocket, programmed some numbers into it, then looked unhappily towards the Kendall-Humes.

Christopher and Margaret remained silent, like schoolchildren fearing the headmaster might ask them a question to which they could not possibly know the answer.

'Come on, come on, how much were you hoping to sting me for?'

'I think you must prepare yourself for a shock, sir,' said the dealer.

'How much?' repeated Kendall-Hume, impatiently.

'Twenty-five thousand.'

'Pounds?'

'Pounds.'

'You must be joking,' said Kendall-Hume, walking round the carpet and ending up standing next to Margaret. 'You're about to find out why I'm considered the scourge of the East Midlands car trade,' he whispered to her. 'I wouldn't pay more than fifteen thousand for that carpet.' He turned back to face the dealer. 'Even if my life depended on it.'

'Then I fear your time has been wasted, sir,' the Turk replied. 'For this is a carpet intended only for the *cognoscenti*. Perhaps madam might reconsider the red and blue?'

'Certainly not,' said Kendall-Hume. 'The colour's all faded. Can't you see? You obviously left it in the window too long, and the sun has got at it. No, you'll have to reconsider your price if you want the orange and yellow one to end up in the home of a connoisseur.'

The dealer sighed as his fingers tapped the calculator again.

While the transaction continued, Melody looked on vacantly, occasionally gazing out of the window towards the bay.

'I could not drop a penny below twenty-three thousand pounds.'

'I'd be willing to go as high as eighteen thousand,' said Kendall-Hume, 'but not a penny more.'

The Roberts watched the dealer tap the numbers into the calculator.

'That would not even cover the cost of what I paid for it myself,' he said sadly, staring down at the little glowing figures.

'You're pushing me, but don't push me too far. Nineteen thousand,' said Mr Kendall-Hume. 'That's my final offer.'

'Twenty thousand pounds is the lowest figure I could consider,' replied the dealer. 'A give-away price on my mother's grave.'

Kendall-Hume took out his wallet and placed it on the table by the side of the dealer.

'Nineteen thousand pounds and you've got yourself a deal,' he said.

'But how will I feed my children?' asked the dealer, his arms raised above his head.

'The same way I feed mine,' said Kendall-Hume, laughing. 'By making a fair profit.'

The dealer paused as if re-considering, then said, 'I can't do it, sir. I'm sorry. We must show you some other carpets.' The assistants came forward on cue.

'No, that's the one I want,' said Mrs Kendall-Hume. 'Don't quarrel over a thousand pounds, pet.'

'Take my word for it, madam,' the dealer said, turning towards Mrs Kendall-Hume. 'My family would starve if we only did business with customers like your husband.'

'Okay, you get the twenty thousand, but on one condition.'

'Condition?'

'My receipt must show that the bill was for ten thousand pounds. Otherwise I'll only end up paying the difference in customs duty.'

The dealer bowed low as if to indicate he did not find the request an unusual one.

Mr Kendall-Hume opened his wallet and withdrew ten thousand pounds in travellers' cheques and ten thousand pounds in cash.

'As you can see,' he said, grinning, 'I came prepared.' He removed another five thousand pounds and, waving it at the dealer, added, 'and I would have been willing to pay far more.'

The dealer shrugged. 'You drive a hard bargain, sir. But you will not hear me complain now the deal has been struck.'

The vast carpet was folded, wrapped and a receipt for ten thousand pounds made out while the travellers' cheques and cash were paid over.

The Roberts had not uttered a word for twenty minutes. When they saw the cash change hands it crossed Margaret's mind that it was more money than the two of them earned in a year.

'Time to get back to the yacht,' said Kendall-Hume. 'Do join us for lunch if you choose a carpet in time.'

'Thank you,' said the Roberts in unison. They waited until the Kendall-Humes were out of sight, two assistants bearing the orange and yellow carpet in their wake, before they thanked the dealer for the coffee and in turn began to make their move towards the door.

'What sort of carpet were you looking for?' asked the dealer.

'I fear your prices are way beyond us,' said Christopher politely. 'But thank you.'

'Well, let me at least find out. Have you or your wife seen a carpet you liked?'

'Yes,' replied Margaret, 'the small carpet, but . . .'

'Ah, yes,' said the dealer. 'I remember madam's eyes when she saw the Hereke.'

He left them, to return a few moments later with the little soft-toned, green-based carpet with the tiny red squares that the Kendall-Humes had so firmly rejected. Not waiting for assistance he rolled it out himself for the Roberts to inspect more carefully.

Margaret thought it looked even more magnificent the second time and feared that she could never hope to find its equal in the few hours left to them.

'Perfect,' she admitted, quite unashamedly.

'Then we have only the price to discuss,' said the dealer kindly. 'How much were you wanting to spend, madam?'

'We had planned to spend three hundred pounds,' said Christopher, jumping in. Margaret was unable to hide her surprise.

'But we agreed –' she began.

'Thank you, my dear, I think I should deal with this matter.'

The dealer smiled and returned to the bargaining.

'I would have to charge you six hundred pounds,' he said. 'Anything less would be robbery.'

'Four hundred pounds is my final offer,' said Christopher, trying to sound in control.

'Five hundred pounds would have to be my bottom price,' said the dealer.

'I'll take it!' cried Christopher.

An assistant began waving his arms and talking to the dealer noisily in his native tongue. The owner raised a hand to dismiss the young man's protests, while the Roberts looked on anxiously.

'My son,' explained the dealer, 'is not happy with the arrangement, but I am delighted that the little carpet will reside in the home of a couple who will so obviously appreciate its true worth.'

'Thank you,' said Christopher quietly.

'Will you also require a bill of a different price?'

'No, thank you,' said Christopher, handing over ten fifty-pound notes and then waiting until the carpet was wrapped and he was presented with the correct receipt.

As he watched the Roberts leave his shop clinging on to their purchase, the dealer smiled to himself.

When they arrived at the quayside, the Kendall-Humes' boat was already half way across the bay heading towards the quiet beach. The Roberts sighed their combined relief and returned to the bazaar for lunch.

It was while they were waiting for their baggage to appear on the carousel at Heathrow Airport that Christopher felt a tap on his shoulder. He turned round to face a beaming Ray Kendall-Hume.

'I wonder if you could do me a favour, old boy?'

'I will if I can,' said Christopher, who still had not fully recovered from their last encounter.

'It's simple enough,' said Kendall-Hume. 'The old girl and I have brought back far too many presents and I wondered if you could take one of them through customs. Otherwise we're likely to be held up all night.'

Melody, standing behind an already laden trolley, smiled at the two men benignly.

'You would still have to pay any duty that was due on it,' said Christopher firmly.

'I wouldn't dream of doing otherwise,' said Kendall-Hume, struggling with a massive package before pushing it on the Roberts' trolley. Christopher wanted to protest as Kendall-Hume peeled off two thousand pounds and handed the money and the receipt over to the schoolmaster.

'What do we do if they claim your carpet is worth a lot more than ten thousand pounds?' asked Margaret anxiously, coming to stand by her husband's side.

'Pay the difference and I'll refund you immediately. But I assure you it's most unlikely to arise.'

'I hope you're right.'

'Of course I'm right,' said Kendall-Hume. 'Don't worry, I've done this sort of thing before. And I won't forget your help when it comes to the next school appeal,' he added, leaving them with the huge parcel.

Once Christopher and Margaret had located their own bags, they collected the second trolley and took their place in the red 'Something to Declare' queue.

'Are you in possession of any items over five hundred pounds in value?' asked the young customs official politely.

'Yes,' said Christopher. 'We purchased two carpets when we were on holiday in Turkey.' He handed over the two bills.

The customs official studied the receipts carefully, then asked if he might be allowed to see the carpets for himself.

'Certainly,' said Christopher, and began the task of undoing the larger package while Margaret worked on the smaller one.

'I shall need to have these looked at by an expert,'

said the official once the parcels were unwrapped. 'It shouldn't take more than a few minutes.' The carpets were soon taken away.

The 'few minutes' turned out to be over fifteen and Christopher and Margaret were soon regretting their decision to assist the Kendall-Humes, whatever the needs of the school appeal. They began to indulge in irrelevant small-talk that wouldn't have fooled the most amateur of sleuths.

At last the customs official returned.

'I wonder if you would be kind enough to have a word with my colleague in private?' he asked.

'Is that really necessary?' asked Christopher, reddening.

'I'm afraid so, sir.'

'We shouldn't have agreed to it in the first place,' whispered Margaret. 'We've never been in any trouble with the authorities before.'

'Don't fret, dear. It will be all over in a few minutes, you'll see,' said Christopher, not sure that he believed his own words. They followed the young man out through the back and into a small room.

'Good afternoon, sir,' said a white-haired man with several gold rings around the cuff of his sleeve. 'I am sorry to have kept you waiting but we have had your carpets looked at by our expert and he feels sure a mistake must have been made.'

Christopher wanted to protest but he couldn't get a word out.

'A mistake?' managed Margaret.

'Yes, madam. The bills you presented don't make any sense to him.'

'Don't make any sense?'

'No, madam,' said the senior customs officer. 'I repeat, we feel certain a mistake has been made.'

'What kind of mistake?' asked Christopher, at last finding his voice.

'Well, you have come forward and declared two carpets, one at a price of ten thousand pounds and one at a price of five hundred pounds, according to these receipts.'

'Yes?'

'Every year hundreds of people return to England with Turkish carpets, so we have some experience in these matters. Our adviser feels certain that the bills have been incorrectly made out.'

'I don't begin to understand . . .' said Christopher.

'Well,' explained the senior officer, 'the large carpet, we are assured, has been spun with a crude distaff and has only two hundred ghiordes, or knots, per square inch. Despite its size we estimate it to be valued around five thousand pounds. The small carpet, on the other hand, we estimate to have nine hundred knots per square inch and is a fine example of a silk hand-woven traditional Hereke and undoubtedly would have been a bargain at five hundred pounds. As both carpets come from the same shop, we assume it must be a clerical error.'

The Roberts remained speechless.

'It doesn't make any difference to the duty you will

have to pay, but we felt sure you would want to know, for insurance purposes.'

Still the Roberts said nothing.

'As you're allowed five hundred pounds before paying any duty, the excise will still be two thousand pounds.'

Christopher quickly handed over the Kendall-Humes' wad of notes. The senior officer counted them while his junior carefully re-wrapped the two carpets.

'Thank you,' said Christopher, as they were handed back the parcels and a receipt for the two thousand pounds.

The Roberts quickly bundled the large package on to its trolley before wheeling it through the concourse and on to the pavement outside where the Kendall-Humes impatiently awaited them.

'You were in there a long time,' said Kendall-Hume. 'Any problems?'

'No, they were just assessing the value of the carpets.'

'Any extra charge?' Kendall-Hume asked apprehensively.

'No, your two thousand pounds covered everything,' said Christopher, passing over the receipt.

'Then we got away with it, old fellow. Well done. One hell of a bargain to add to my collection.' Kendall-Hume turned to bundle the large package into the boot of his Mercedes before locking it and taking his place behind the steering wheel. 'Well done,' he repeated through the open window, as the car drove off. 'I won't forget the school appeal.'

The Roberts stood and watched as the silver grey car joined a line of traffic leaving the airport.

'Why didn't you tell Mr Kendall-Hume the real value of his carpet?' asked Margaret once they were seated in the bus.

'I did give it some considerable thought but I came to the conclusion that the *truth* was the last thing Kendall-Hume wanted to be told.'

'But don't you feel any guilt? After all, we've stolen –'

'Not at all, my dear. We haven't stolen anything. But we did get one hell of a "steal".'

COLONEL BULLFROG

THERE IS ONE cathedral in England that has never found it necessary to launch a national appeal.

When the Colonel woke he found himself tied to a stake where the ambush had taken place. He could feel a numb sensation in his leg. The last thing he could recall was the bayonet entering his thigh. All he was aware of now were ants crawling up the leg on an endless march towards the wound.

It would have been better to have remained unconscious, he decided.

Then someone undid the knots and he collapsed head first into the mud. It would be better still to be dead, he concluded. The Colonel somehow got to his knees and crawled over to the stake next to him. Tied to it was a corporal who must have been dead for several hours. Ants were crawling into his mouth. The Colonel tore off a strip from the man's shirt, washed it in a large puddle nearby and cleaned the wound in his leg as best he could before binding it tightly.

That was February 17th, 1943, a date that would

be etched on the Colonel's memory for the rest of his life.

That same morning the Japanese received orders that the newly captured Allied prisoners were to be moved at dawn. Many were to die on the march and even more had perished before the trek began. Colonel Richard Moore was determined not to be counted among them.

Twenty-nine days later, one hundred and seventeen of the original seven hundred and thirty-two Allied troops reached Tonchan. Any man whose travels had previously not taken him beyond Rome could hardly have been prepared for such an experience as Tonchan. This heavily guarded prisoner-of-war camp, some three hundred miles north of Singapore and hidden in the deepest equatorial jungle, offered no possibility of freedom. Anyone who contemplated escape could not hope to survive in the jungle for more than a few days, while those who remained discovered the odds were not a lot shorter.

When the Colonel first arrived, Major Sakata, the camp commandant, informed him that he was the senior ranking officer and would therefore be held responsible for the welfare of all Allied troops.

Colonel Moore had stared down at the Japanese officer. Sakata must have been a foot shorter than himself but after that twenty-eight-day march the British soldier couldn't have weighed much more than the diminutive Major.

Moore's first act on leaving the commandant's

Colonel Bullfrog

office was to call together all the Allied officers. He discovered there was a good cross-section from Britain, Australia, New Zealand and America but few could have been described as fit. Men were dying daily from malaria, dysentery and malnutrition. He was suddenly aware what the expression 'dying like flies' meant.

The Colonel learned from his staff officers that for the previous two years of the camp's existence they had been ordered to build bamboo huts for the Japanese officers. These had had to be completed before they had been allowed to start on a hospital for their own men and only recently huts for themselves. Many prisoners had died during those two years, not from illness but from the atrocities some Japanese perpetrated on a daily basis. Major Sakata, known because of his skinny arms as 'Chopsticks', was, however, not considered to be the villain. His second-in-command, Lieutenant Takasaki (the Undertaker), and Sergeant Ayut (the Pig) were of a different mould and to be avoided at all cost, his men warned him.

It took the Colonel only a few days to discover why.

He decided his first task was to try to raise the battered morale of his troops. As there was no padre among those officers who had been captured he began each day by conducting a short service of prayer. Once the service was over the men would start work on the railway that ran alongside the camp. Each arduous day consisted of laying tracks to help Japanese soldiers get to the front more quickly so they could in turn kill and capture more Allied troops. Any prisoner suspected of undermining this work was found guilty of sabotage and put to death without trial. Lieutenant Takasaki considered taking an unscheduled five-minute break to be sabotage.

At lunch prisoners were allowed twenty minutes off to share a bowl of rice – usually with maggots – and, if they were lucky, a mug of water. Although the men returned to the camp each night exhausted, the Colonel still set about organising squads to be responsible for the cleanliness of their huts and the state of the latrines.

After only a few months, the Colonel was able to organise a football match between the British and the Americans, and following its success even set up a camp league. But he was even more delighted when the men turned up for karate lessons under Sergeant Hawke, a thick-set Australian, who had a Black Belt and for good measure also played the mouth-organ. The tiny instrument had survived the march through the jungle but everyone assumed it would be discovered before long and confiscated.

Each day Moore renewed his determination not to allow the Japanese to believe for one moment that the Allies were beaten – despite the fact that while he was at Tonchan he lost another twenty pounds in weight, and at least one man under his command every day.

To the Colonel's surprise the camp commandant, despite the Japanese national belief that any soldier who allowed himself to be captured ought to be treated as a deserter, did not place too many unnecessary obstacles in his path.

'You are like the British Bullfrog,' Major Sakata suggested one evening as he watched the Colonel carving cricket bails out of bamboo. It was one of the rare occasions when the Colonel managed a smile.

His real problems continued to come from Lieutenant Takasaki and his henchmen, who considered captured Allied prisoners fit only to be considered as traitors. Takasaki was always careful how he treated the Colonel personally, but felt no such reservations when dealing with the other ranks, with the result that Allied soldiers often ended up with their meagre rations confiscated, a rifle butt in the stomach, or even left bound to a tree for days on end.

Whenever the Colonel made an official complaint to the commandant, Major Sakata listened sympathetically and even made an effort to weed out the main offenders. Moore's happiest moment at Tonchan was to witness the Undertaker and the Pig boarding the train for the front line. No one attempted to sabotage that journey. The commandant replaced them with Sergeant Akida and Corporal Sushi, known by the prisoners almost affectionately as 'Sweet and Sour Pork'. However, the Japanese High Command sent a new Number Two to the camp, a Lieutenant Osawa, who quickly became known as 'The Devil' since he perpetrated atrocities that made the Undertaker and the Pig look like church fête organisers.

As the months passed the Colonel and the commandant's mutual respect grew. Sakata even confided to his English prisoner that he had requested that he be sent to the front line and join the real war. 'And if,' the Major added, 'the High Command grants my request, there will be only two NCOs I would want to accompany me.'

Colonel Moore knew the Major had Sweet and Sour Pork in mind, and was fearful what might become of his men if the only three Japanese he could work with were posted back to active duties to leave Lieutenant Osawa in command of the camp.

Colonel Moore realised that something quite extraordinary must have taken place for Major Sakata to come to his hut, because he had never done so before. The Colonel put his bowl of rice back down on the table and asked the three Allied officers who were sharing breakfast with him to wait outside.

The Major stood to attention and saluted.

The Colonel pushed himself to his full six feet, returned the salute and stared down into Sakata's eyes.

'The war is over,' said the Japanese officer. For a brief moment Moore feared the worst. 'Japan has surrendered unconditionally. You, sir,' Sakata said quietly, 'are now in command of the camp.'

The Colonel immediately ordered all Japanese

officers to be placed under arrest in the command-ant's quarters. While his orders were being carried out he personally went in search of The Devil. Moore marched across the parade ground and headed towards the officers' quarters. He located the second-in-command's hut, walked up the steps and threw open Osawa's door. The sight that met the new com-mandant's eyes was one he would never forget. The Colonel had read of ceremonial hara-kiri without any real idea of what the final act consisted. Lieutenant Osawa must have cut himself a hundred times before he eventually died. The blood, the stench and the sight of the mutilated body would have caused a Gurkha to be sick. Only the head was there to confirm that the remains had once belonged to a human being.

The Colonel ordered Osawa to be buried outside the gates of the camp.

When the surrender of Japan was finally signed on board the US *Missouri* in Tokyo Bay, all at Tonchan PoW camp listened to the ceremony on the single camp radio. Colonel Moore then called a full parade on the camp square. For the first time in two and a half years he wore his dress uniform which made him look like a pierrot who had turned up at a formal party. He accepted the Japanese flag of surrender from Major Sakata on behalf of the Allies, then made the defeated enemy raise the American and British flags to the sound of both national anthems played in turn by Sergeant Hawke on his mouth-organ.

The Colonel then held a short service of thanksgiving which he conducted in the presence of all the Allied and Japanese soldiers.

Once command had changed hands Colonel Moore waited as week followed pointless week for news that he would be sent home. Many of his men had been given their orders to start the ten-thousand-mile journey back to England via Bangkok and Calcutta, but no such orders came for the Colonel and he waited in vain to be sent his repatriation papers.

Then, in January 1946, a smartly dressed young Guards officer arrived at the camp with orders to see the Colonel. He was conducted to the commandant's office and saluted before shaking hands. Richard Moore stared at the young captain who, from his healthy complexion, had obviously arrived in the Far East long after the Japanese had surrendered. The captain handed over a letter to the Colonel.

'Home at last,' said the older man breezily, as he ripped open the envelope, only to discover that it would be years before he could hope to exchange the paddy fields of Tonchan for the green fields of Lincolnshire.

The letter requested that the Colonel travel to Tokyo and represent Britain on the forthcoming war tribunal which was to be conducted in the Japanese capital. Captain Ross of the Coldstream Guards would take over his command at Tonchan.

The tribunal was to consist of twelve officers under the chairmanship of General Matthew Tomkins. Moore was to be the sole British representative and was to report directly to the General, 'as soon as you find it convenient'. Further details would be supplied to him on his arrival in Tokyo. The letter ended: 'If for any reason you should require my help in your deliberations, do not hesitate to contact me personally.' There followed the signature of Clement Attlee.

Staff officers are not in the habit of disobeying Prime Ministers, so the Colonel resigned himself to a prolonged stay in Japan.

It took several months to set up the tribunal and during that time Colonel Moore continued supervising the return of British troops to their homeland. The paperwork was endless and some of the men under his command were so frail that he found it necessary to build them up spiritually as well as physically before he could put them on boats to their various destinations. Some died long after the declaration of surrender had been ratified.

During this period of waiting, Colonel Moore used Major Sakata and the two NCOs in whom he had placed so much trust, Sergeant Akida and Corporal Sushi, as his liaison officers. This sudden change of command did not affect the relationship

between the two senior officers, although Sakata
admitted to the Colonel that he wished he had been
killed in the defence of his country and not left to
witness its humiliations. The Colonel found the
Japanese remained well-disciplined while they waited
to learn their fate, and most of them assumed death
was the natural consequence of defeat.

The war tribunal held its first plenary session in Tokyo
on April 19th, 1946. General Tomkins took over the
fifth floor of the old Imperial Courthouse in the Ginza
quarter of Tokyo – one of the few buildings that had
survived the war intact. Tomkins, a squat, short-
tempered man who was described by his own staff
officer as a 'pen-pusher from the Pentagon', arrived
in Tokyo only a week before he began his first
deliberations. The only rat-a-tat-tat this General had
ever heard, the staff officer freely admitted to Colonel
Moore, had come from the typewriter in his secretary's office. However, when it came to those on
trial the General was in no doubt as to where the guilt
lay and how the guilty should be punished.

'Hang every one of the little slit-eyed, yellow
bastards,' turned out to be one of Tomkins's favourite
expressions.

Seated round a table in an old courtroom, the
twelve-man tribunal conducted their deliberations. It
was clear from the opening session that the General
had no intention of considering 'extenuating circum-

stances', 'past record' or 'humanitarian grounds'. As the Colonel listened to Tomkins's views he began to fear for the lives of any innocent member of the armed forces who was brought in front of the General.

The Colonel quickly identified four Americans from the tribunal who, like himself, did not always concur with the General's sweeping judgments. Two were lawyers and the other two had been fighting soldiers recently involved in combat duty. The five men began to work together to counteract the General's most prejudiced decisions. During the following weeks they were able to persuade one or two others around the table to commute the sentences of hanging to life imprisonment for several Japanese who had been condemned for crimes they could not possibly have committed.

As each such case was debated, General Tomkins left the five men in no doubt as to his contempt for their views. 'Goddam Nip sympathisers,' he often suggested, and not always under his breath. As the General still held sway over the twelve-man tribunal, the Colonel's successes turned out to be few in number.

When the time came to determine the fate of those who had been in command of the PoW camp at Tonchan the General demanded mass hanging for every Japanese officer involved without even the pretence of a proper trial. He showed no surprise when the usual five tribunal members raised their voices in protest. Colonel Moore spoke eloquently of having been a prisoner at Tonchan and petitioned in the defence of Major Sakata, Sergeant Akida and Corporal Sushi. He attempted to explain why hanging them would in its own way be as barbaric as any atrocity carried out by the Japanese. He insisted their sentence should be commuted to life imprisonment. The General yawned throughout the Colonel's remarks and, once Moore had completed his case, made no attempt to justify his position but simply called for a vote. To the General's surprise, the result was six-all; an American lawyer who previously had sided with the General raised his hand to join the Colonel's five. Without hesitation the General threw his casting vote in favour of the gallows. Tomkins leered down the table at Moore and said, 'Time for lunch, I think, gentlemen. I don't know about you but I'm famished. And no one can say that this time we didn't give the little yellow bastards a fair hearing.'

Colonel Moore rose from his place and without offering an opinion left the room.

He ran down the steps of the courthouse and instructed his driver to take him to British HQ in the centre of the city as quickly as possible. The short journey took them some time because of the mêlée of people that were always thronging the streets night and day. Once the Colonel arrived at his office he asked his secretary to place a call through to England. While she was carrying out his order Moore went to his green cabinet and thumbed through several files until he reached the one marked 'Personal'. He opened it and fished out the letter. He wanted to be certain that he had remembered the sentence accurately . . .

'If for any reason you should require my help in your deliberations, do not hesitate to contact me personally.'

'He's coming to the phone, sir,' the secretary said nervously. The Colonel walked over to the phone and waited. He found himself standing to attention when he heard the gentle, cultivated voice ask, 'Is that you, Colonel?' It took Richard Moore less than ten minutes to explain the problem he faced and obtain the authority he needed.

Immediately he had completed his conversation he returned to the tribunal headquarters. He marched straight back into the conference room just as General Tomkins was settling down in his chair to start the afternoon proceedings.

The Colonel was the first to rise from his place when the General declared the tribunal to be in session. 'I wonder if I might be allowed to open with a statement?' he requested.

'Be my guest,' said Tomkins. 'But make it brief. We've got a lot more of these Japs to get through yet.'

Colonel Moore looked around the table at the other eleven men.

'Gentlemen,' he began. 'I hereby resign my position as the British representative on this commission.'

General Tomkins was unable to stifle a smile.

'I do it,' the Colonel continued, 'reluctantly, but

with the backing of my Prime Minister, to whom I spoke only a few moments ago.' At this piece of information Tomkins's smile was replaced by a frown. 'I shall be returning to England in order to make a full report to Mr Attlee and the British Cabinet on the manner in which this tribunal is being conducted.'

'Now look here, sonny,' began the General. 'You can't –'

'I can, sir, and I will. Unlike you, I am unwilling to have the blood of innocent soldiers on my hands for the rest of my life.'

'Now look here, sonny,' the General repeated. 'Let's at least talk this through before you do anything you might regret.'

There was no break for the rest of that day, and by late afternoon Major Sakata, Sergeant Akida and Corporal Sushi had had their sentences commuted to life imprisonment.

Within a month, General Tomkins had been recalled by the Pentagon to be replaced by a distinguished American marine who had been decorated in combat during the First World War.

In the weeks that followed the new appointment the death sentences of two hundred and twenty-nine Japanese prisoners of war were commuted.

Colonel Moore returned to Lincolnshire on November 11th, 1948, having had enough of the realities of war and the hypocrisies of peace.

*

Just under two years later Richard Moore took holy orders and became a parish priest in the sleepy hamlet of Weddlebeach, in Suffolk. He enjoyed his calling and although he rarely mentioned his wartime experiences to his parishioners he often thought of his days in Japan.

'Blessed are the peacemakers for they shall . . .' the vicar began his sermon from the pulpit one Palm Sunday morning in the early 1960s, but he failed to complete the sentence.

His parishioners looked up anxiously only to see that a broad smile had spread across the vicar's face as he gazed down at someone seated in the third row.

The man he was staring at bowed his head in embarrassment and the vicar quickly continued with his sermon.

When the service was over Richard Moore waited by the east door to be sure his eyes had not deceived him. When they met face to face for the first time in fifteen years both men bowed and then shook hands.

The priest was delighted to learn over lunch that day back at the vicarage that Chopsticks Sakata had been released from prison after only five years, following the Allies' agreement with the newly installed Japanese government to release all prisoners who had not committed capital crimes. When the Colonel enquired after 'Sweet and Sour Pork' the Major admitted that he had lost touch with Sergeant Akida (Sweet) but that Corporal Sushi (Sour) and he were working for the same electronics company. 'And whenever we meet,' he assured the priest, 'we talk of the honourable man who saved our lives, "the British Bullfrog".'

Over the years, the priest and his Japanese friend progressed in their chosen professions and regularly corresponded with each other. In 1971 Ari Sakata was put in charge of a large electronics factory in Osaka while eighteen months later Richard Moore became the Very Revd Richard Moore, Dean of Lincoln Cathedral.

'I read in the London *Times* that your cathedral is appealing for a new roof,' wrote Sakata from his homeland in 1975.

'Nothing unusual about that,' the Dean explained in his letter of reply. 'There isn't a cathedral in England that doesn't suffer from dry rot or bomb damage. The former I fear is terminal; the latter at least has the chance of a cure.'

A few weeks later the Dean received a cheque for ten thousand pounds from a not-unknown Japanese electronics company.

When in 1979 the Very Revd Richard Moore was appointed to the bishopric of Taunton, the new managing director of the largest electronics company in Japan flew over to attend his enthronement.

'I see you have another roof problem,' commented Ari Sakata as he gazed up at the scaffolding surrounding the pulpit. 'How much will it cost this time?'

'At least twenty-five thousand pounds a year,'

replied the Bishop without thought. 'Just to make sure the roof doesn't fall in on the congregation during my sterner sermons.' He sighed as he passed the evidence of reconstruction all around him. 'As soon as I've settled into my new job I intend to launch a proper appeal to ensure my successor doesn't have to worry about the roof ever again.'

The managing director nodded his understanding. A week later a cheque for twenty-five thousand pounds arrived on the churchman's desk.

The Bishop tried hard to express his grateful thanks. He knew he must never allow Chopsticks to feel that by his generosity he might have done the wrong thing as this would only insult his friend and undoubtedly end their relationship. Rewrite after rewrite was drafted to ensure that the final version of the long hand-written letter would have passed muster with the Foreign Office mandarin in charge of the Japanese desk. Finally the letter was posted.

As the years passed Richard Moore became fearful of writing to his old friend more than once a year as each letter elicited an even larger cheque. And, when towards the end of 1986 he did write, he made no reference to the Dean and Chapter's decision to designate 1988 as the cathedral's appeal year. Nor did he mention his own failing health, lest the old Japanese gentleman should feel in some way responsible, as his doctor had warned him that he could never expect to recover fully from those experiences at Tonchan.

The Bishop set about forming his appeal committee in January 1987. The Prince of Wales became the patron and the Lord Lieutenant of the county its chairman. In his opening address to the members of the appeal committee the Bishop instructed them that it was their duty to raise not less than three million pounds during 1988. Some apprehensive looks appeared on the faces around the table.

On August 11th, 1987, the Bishop of Taunton was umpiring a village cricket match when he suddenly collapsed from a heart attack. 'See that the appeal brochures are printed in time for the next meeting,' were his final words to the captain of the local team.

Bishop Moore's memorial service was held in Taunton Cathedral and conducted by the Archbishop of Canterbury. Not a seat could be found in the cathedral that day, and so many crowded into every pew that the west door was left open. Those who arrived late had to listen to the Archbishop's address relayed over loudspeakers placed around the market square.

Casual onlookers must have been puzzled by the presence of several elderly Japanese gentlemen dotted around the congregation.

When the service came to an end the Archbishop held a private meeting in the vestry of the cathedral with the chairman of the largest electronics company in the world.

'You must be Mr Sakata,' said the Archbishop, warmly shaking the hand of a man who stepped forward from the small cluster of Japanese who were in attendance. 'Thank you for taking the trouble to write and let me know that you would be coming. I am delighted to meet you at last. The Bishop always spoke of you with great affection and as a close friend – "Chopsticks", if I remember.'

Mr Sakata bowed low.

'And I also know that he always considered himself in your personal debt for such generosity over so many years.'

'No, no, not me,' replied the former Major. 'I, like my dear friend the late Bishop, am representative of higher authority.'

The Archbishop looked puzzled.

'You see, sir,' continued Mr Sakata, 'I am only the chairman of the company. May I have the honour of introducing my President?'

Mr Sakata took a pace backwards to allow an even smaller figure, whom the Archbishop had originally assumed to be part of Mr Sakata's entourage, to step forward.

The President bowed low and, still without speaking, passed an envelope to the Archbishop.

'May I be allowed to open it?' the church leader asked, unaware of the Japanese custom of waiting until the giver has departed.

The little man bowed again.

The Archbishop slit open the envelope and removed a cheque for three million pounds.

'The late Bishop must have been a very close friend,' was all he could think of saying.

'No, sir,' the President replied. 'I did not have that privilege.'

'Then he must have done something incredible to be deserving of such a munificent gesture.'

'He performed an act of honour over forty years ago and now I try inadequately to repay it.'

'Then he would surely have remembered you,' said the Archbishop.

'Is possible he would remember me but if so only as the sour half of "Sweet and Sour Pork".'

There is one cathedral in England that has never found it necessary to launch a national appeal.

CHECKMATE

As SHE ENTERED the room every eye turned towards her.

When admiring a girl some men start with her head and work down. I start with the ankles and work up.

She wore black high-heeled velvet shoes and a tight-fitting black dress that stopped high enough above the knees to reveal the most perfectly tapering legs. As my eyes continued their upward sweep they paused to take in her narrow waist and slim athletic figure. But it was the oval face that I found captivating, slightly pouting lips and the largest blue eyes I've ever seen, crowned with a head of thick, black, short-cut hair that literally shone with lustre. Her entrance was all the more breathtaking because of the surroundings she had chosen. Heads would have turned at a diplomatic reception, a society cocktail party, even a charity ball, but at a chess tournament . . .

I followed her every movement, patronisingly unable to accept she could be a player. She walked slowly over to the club secretary's table and signed in to prove me wrong. She was handed a number to indicate her challenger for the opening match. Anyone who had not yet been allocated an opponent waited to see if she would take her place opposite their side of the board.

The player checked the number she had been given and made her way towards an elderly man who was seated in the far corner of the room, a former captain of the club now past his best.

As the club's new captain I had been responsible for instigating these round-robin matches. We meet on the last Friday of the month in a large club-like room on top of the Mason's Arms in the High Street. The landlord sees to it that thirty tables are set out for us and that food and drink are readily available. Three or four other clubs in the district send half a dozen opponents to play a couple of blitz games, giving us a chance to face rivals we would not normally play. The rules for the matches are simple enough – one minute on the clock is the maximum allowed for each move, so a game rarely lasts for more than an hour, and if a pawn hasn't been captured in thirty moves the game is automatically declared a draw. A short break for a drink between games, paid for by the loser, ensures that everyone has the chance to challenge two opponents during the evening.

A thin man wearing half-moon spectacles and a dark blue three-piece suit made his way over towards my board. We smiled and shook hands. My guess would have been a solicitor, but I was wrong as he turned out to be an accountant working for a stationery supplier in Woking.

I found it hard to concentrate on my opponent's well-rehearsed Moscow opening as my eyes kept leaving the board and wandering over to the girl in the black dress. On the one occasion our eyes did meet she gave me an enigmatic smile, but although I tried again I was unable to elicit the same response a second time. Despite being preoccupied I still managed to defeat the accountant, who seemed unaware that there were several ways out of a seven-pawn attack.

At the half-time break three other members of the club had offered her a drink before I even reached the bar. I knew I could not hope to play my second match against the girl as I would be expected to challenge one of the visiting team captains. In fact she ended up playing the accountant.

I defeated my new opponent in a little over forty minutes and, as a solicitous host, began to take an interest in the other matches that were still being played. I set out on a circuitous route that ensured I ended up at her table. I could see that the accountant already had the better of her and within moments of my arrival she had lost both her queen and the game.

I introduced myself and found that just shaking hands with her was a sexual experience. Weaving our way through the tables we strolled over to the bar together. Her name, she told me, was Amanda Curzon. I ordered Amanda the glass of red wine she requested and a half-pint of beer for myself. I began by commiserating with her over the defeat.

'How did you get on against him?' she asked.

'Just managed to beat him,' I said. 'But it was very close. How did your first game with our old captain turn out?'

'Stalemate,' said Amanda. 'But I think he was just being courteous.'

'Last time I played him it ended up in stalemate,' I told her.

She smiled. 'Perhaps we ought to have a game some time?'

'I'll look forward to that,' I said, as she finished her drink.

'Well, I must be off,' she announced suddenly. 'Have to catch the last train to Hounslow.'

'Allow me to drive you,' I said gallantly. 'It's the least the host captain can be expected to do.'

'But surely it's miles out of your way?'

'Not at all,' I lied, Hounslow being about twenty minutes beyond my flat. I gulped down the last drop of my beer and helped Amanda on with her coat. Before leaving I thanked the landlord for the efficient organisation of the evening.

We then strolled into the car park. I opened the passenger door of my Scirocco to allow Amanda to climb in.

'A slight improvement on London Transport,' she said as I slid into my side of the car. I smiled and headed out on the road northwards. That black dress that I described earlier goes even higher up the legs when a girl sits back in a Scirocco. It didn't seem to embarrass her.

'It's still very early,' I ventured after a few inconsequential remarks about the club evening. 'Have you time to drop in for a drink?'

'It would have to be a quick one,' she replied, looking at her watch. 'I've a busy day ahead of me tomorrow.'

'Of course,' I said, chatting on, hoping she wouldn't notice a detour that could hardly be described as on the way to Hounslow.

'Do you work in town?' I asked.

'Yes. I'm a receptionist for a firm of estate agents in Berkeley Square.'

'I'm surprised you're not a model.'

'I used to be,' she replied without further explanation. She seemed quite oblivious to the route I was taking as she chatted on about her holiday plans for Ibiza. Once we had arrived at my place I parked the car and led Amanda through my front gate and up to the flat. In the hall I helped her off with her coat before taking her through to the front room.

'What would you like to drink?' I asked.

'I'll stick to wine, if you've a bottle already open,' she replied, as she walked slowly round, taking in the unusually tidy room. My mother must have dropped by during the morning, I thought gratefully.

'It's only a bachelor pad,' I said, emphasising the word 'bachelor' before going into the kitchen. To my relief I found there was an unopened bottle of wine in the larder. I joined Amanda with the bottle and two glasses a few moments later, to find her studying my chess board and fingering the delicate ivory pieces that were set out for a game I was playing by post.

'What a beautiful set,' she volunteered as I handed her a glass of wine. 'Where did you find it?'

'Mexico,' I told her, not explaining that I had won it in a tournament while on holiday there. 'I was only sorry we didn't have the chance to have a game ourselves.'

She checked her watch. 'Time for a quick one,' she said, taking a seat behind the little white pieces.

I quickly took my place opposite her. She smiled, picked up a white and a black bishop and hid them behind her back. Her dress became even tighter and emphasised the shape of her breasts. She then placed both clenched fists in front of me. I touched her right hand and she turned it over and opened it to reveal a white bishop.

'Is there to be a wager of any kind?' I asked lightheartedly. She checked inside her evening bag.

'I only have a few pounds on me,' she said.

'I'd be willing to play for lower stakes.'

'What do you have in mind?' she asked.

'What can you offer?'

'What would you like?'

'Ten pounds if you win.'

'And if I lose?'

'You take something off.'

I regretted the words the moment I had said them and waited for her to slap my face and leave but she said simply, 'There's not much harm in that if we only play one game.'

I nodded my agreement and stared down at the board.

She wasn't a bad player – what the pros call a *patzer* – though her Roux opening was somewhat orthodox. I managed to make the game last twenty minutes while sacrificing several pieces without making it look too obvious. When I said 'Checkmate', she kicked off both her shoes and laughed.

'Care for another drink?' I asked, not feeling too hopeful. 'After all, it's not yet eleven.'

'All right. Just a small one and then I must be off.'

I went to the kitchen, returned a moment later clutching the bottle, and refilled her glass.

'I only wanted half a glass,' she said, frowning.

'I was lucky to win,' I said, ignoring her remark, 'after your bishop captured my knight. Extremely close-run thing.'

'Perhaps,' she replied.

'Care for another game?' I ventured.

She hesitated.

'Double or quits?'

'What do you mean?'

'Twenty pounds or another garment?'

'Neither of us is going to lose much tonight, are we?'

She pulled up her chair as I turned the board

A Twist in the Tale

round and we both began to put the ivory pieces back in place.

The second game took a little longer as I made a silly mistake early on, castling on my queen's side, and it took several moves to recover. However, I still managed to finish the game off in under thirty minutes and even found time to refill Amanda's glass when she wasn't looking.

She smiled at me as she hitched her dress up high enough to allow me to see the tops of her stockings. She undid the suspenders and slowly peeled the stockings off before dropping them on my side of the table.

'I nearly beat you that time,' she said.

'Almost,' I replied. 'Want another chance to get even? Let's say fifty pounds this time,' I suggested, trying to make the offer sound magnanimous.

'The stakes are getting higher for both of us,' she replied as she reset the board. I began to wonder what might be going through her mind. Whatever it was, she foolishly sacrificed both her rooks early on and the game was over in a matter of minutes.

Once again she lifted her dress but this time well above her waist. My eyes were glued to her thighs as she undid the black suspender belt and held it high above my head before letting it drop and join her stockings on my side of the table.

'Once I had lost the second rook,' she said, 'I was never in with a chance.'

'I agree. It would therefore only be fair to allow

you one more chance,' I said, quickly re-setting the board. 'After all,' I added, 'you could win one hundred pounds this time.' She smiled.

'I really ought to be going home,' she said as she moved her queen's pawn two squares forward. She smiled that enigmatic smile again as I countered with my bishop's pawn.

It was the best game she had played all evening and her use of the Warsaw gambit kept me at the board for over thirty minutes. In fact I damn nearly lost early on because I found it hard to concentrate properly on her defence strategy. A couple of times Amanda chuckled when she thought she had got the better of me, but it became obvious she had not seen Karpov play the Sicilian defence and win from a seemingly impossible position.

'Checkmate,' I finally declared.

'Damn,' she said, and standing up turned her back on me. 'You'll have to give me a hand.' Trembling, I leaned over and slowly pulled the zip down until it reached the small of her back. Once again I wanted to touch the smooth, creamy skin. She swung round to face me, shrugged gracefully and the dress fell to the ground as if a statue were being unveiled. She leaned forward and brushed the side of my cheek with her hand, which had much the same effect as an electric shock. I emptied the last of the bottle of wine into her glass and left for the kitchen with the excuse of needing to refill my own. When I returned she hadn't moved. A gauzy black bra and pair of panties were now the only garments that I still hoped to see removed.

'I don't suppose you'd play one more game?' I asked, trying not to sound desperate.

'It's time you took me home,' she said with a giggle.

I passed her another glass of wine. 'Just one more,' I begged. 'But this time it must be for both garments.'

She laughed. 'Certainly not,' she said. 'I couldn't afford to lose.'

'It would have to be the last game,' I agreed. 'But two hundred pounds this time and we play for both garments.' I waited, hoping the size of the wager would tempt her. 'The odds must surely be on your side. After all, you've nearly won three times.'

She sipped her drink as if considering the proposition. 'All right,' she said. 'One last fling.'

Neither of us voiced our feeling as to what was certain to happen if she lost.

I could not stop myself trembling as I set the board up once again. I cleared my mind, hoping she hadn't noticed that I had drunk only one glass of wine all night. I was determined to finish this one off quickly.

I moved my queen's pawn one square forward. She retaliated, pushing her king's pawn up two squares. I knew exactly what my next move needed to be and because of it the game only lasted eleven minutes.

I have never been so comprehensively beaten in my life. Amanda was in a totally different class to me. She anticipated my every move and had gambits I had never encountered or even read of before.

It was her turn to say 'Checkmate', which she delivered with the same enigmatic smile as before, adding, 'You did say the odds were on my side this time.'

I lowered my head in disbelief. When I looked up again, she had already slipped that beautiful black dress back on, and was stuffing her stockings and suspenders into her evening bag. A moment later she put on her shoes.

I took out my cheque book, filled in the name 'Amanda Curzon' and added the figure '£200', the date and my signature. While I was doing this she replaced the little ivory pieces on the exact squares on which they had been when she had first entered the room.

She bent over and kissed me gently on the cheek. 'Thank you,' she said as she placed the cheque in her handbag. 'We must play again some time.' I was still staring at the re-set board in disbelief when I heard the front door close behind her.

'Wait a minute,' I said, rushing to the door. 'How will you get home?'

I was just in time to see her running down the steps and towards the open door of a BMW. She climbed in, allowing me one more look at those long tapering legs. She smiled as the car door was closed behind her.

The accountant strolled round to the driver's side, got in, revved up the engine and drove the champion home.

THE WINE TASTER

THE FIRST OCCASION I MET Sefton Hamilton was in late August last year when my wife and I were dining with Henry and Suzanne Kennedy at their home in Warwick Square.

Hamilton was one of those unfortunate men who have inherited immense wealth but not a lot more. He was able quickly to convince us that he had little time to read and no time to attend the theatre or opera. However, this did not prevent him from holding opinions on every subject from Shaw to Pavarotti, from Gorbachev to Picasso. He remained puzzled, for instance, as to what the unemployed had to complain about when their dole packet was only just less than what he was currently paying the labourers on his estate. In any case, they only spent it on bingo and drinking, he assured us.

Drinking brings me to the other dinner guest that night – Freddie Barker, the President of the Wine Society, who sat opposite my wife and unlike Hamilton hardly uttered a word. Henry had assured me over the phone that Barker had not only managed to get the Society back on to a proper financial footing but was also acknowledged as a leading authority on his subject. I looked forward to picking up useful bits of inside knowledge. Whenever Barker was allowed to get a word in edgeways, he showed enough knowledge of the topic under discussion to convince me that he would be fascinating if only Hamilton would remain silent long enough for him to speak.

While our hostess produced as a starter a spinach soufflé that melted in the mouth, Henry moved round the table pouring each of us a glass of wine.

Barker sniffed his appreciatively. 'Appropriate in bicentennial year that we should be drinking an Australian Chablis of such fine vintage. I feel sure their whites will soon be making the French look to their laurels.'

'Australian?' said Hamilton in disbelief as he put down his glass. 'How could a nation of beer-swiggers begin to understand the first thing about producing a half decent wine?'

'I think you'll find,' began Barker, 'that the Australians –'

'Bicentennial indeed,' Hamilton continued. 'Let's face it, they're only celebrating two hundred years of parole.' No one laughed except Hamilton. 'I'd still pack the rest of our criminals off there, given half a chance.'

No one doubted him.

Hamilton sipped the wine tentatively, like a man who fears he is about to be poisoned, then began to explain why, in his considered view, judges were far too lenient with petty criminals. I found myself concentrating more on the food than the incessant flow of my neighbour's views.

I always enjoy Beef Wellington, and Suzanne can produce a pastry that doesn't flake when cut and meat that's so tender that once one has finished a first helping, Oliver Twist comes to mind. It certainly helped me to endure Hamilton's pontificating. Barker managed to pass an appreciative comment to Henry on the quality of the claret between Hamilton's opinions on the chances of Paddy Ashdown reviving the Liberal Party and the role of Arthur Scargill in the trade union movement, allowing no one the chance to reply.

'I don't allow my staff to belong to any union,' Hamilton declared, gulping down his drink. 'I run a closed shop.' He laughed once more at his own joke and held his empty glass high in the air as if it would be filled by magic. In fact it was filled by Henry with a discretion that shamed Hamilton – not that he noticed. In the brief pause that followed, my wife suggested that perhaps the trade union movement had been born out of a response to a genuine social need.

'Balderdash, madam,' said Hamilton. 'With great respect, the trade unions have been the single most important factor in the decline of Britain as we know it. They've no interest in anybody but themselves. You only have to look at Ron Todd and the whole Ford fiasco to understand that.'

Suzanne began to clear the plates away and I

noticed she took the opportunity to nudge Henry, who quickly changed the subject.

Moments later a raspberry meringue glazed with a thick sauce appeared. It seemed a pity to cut such a creation but Suzanne carefully divided six generous helpings like a nanny feeding her charges while Henry uncorked a 1981 Sauternes. Barker literally licked his lips in anticipation.

'And another thing,' Hamilton was saying. 'The Prime Minister has got far too many Wets in her Cabinet for my liking.'

'With whom would you replace them?' asked Barker innocently.

Herod would have had little trouble in convincing the list of gentlemen Hamilton proffered that the slaughter of the innocents was merely an extension of the child care programme.

Once again I became more interested in Suzanne's culinary efforts, especially as she had allowed me an indulgence: Cheddar was to be served as the final course. I knew the moment I tasted it that it had been purchased from the Alvis Brothers' farm in Keynsham; we all have to be knowledgeable about something, and Cheddar is my speciality.

To accompany the cheese, Henry supplied a port which was to be the highlight of the evening. 'Sandeman 1970,' he said in an aside to Barker as he poured the first drops into the expert's glass.

'Yes, of course,' said Barker, holding it to his nose. 'I would have known it anywhere. Typical Sandeman warmth but with real body. I hope you've laid some down, Henry,' he added. 'You'll enjoy it even more in your old age.'

'Think you're a bit of an authority on wines, do you?' said Hamilton, the first question he had asked all evening.

'Not exactly,' began Barker, 'but I –'

'You're all a bunch of humbugs, the lot of you,' interrupted Hamilton. 'You sniff and you swirl, you taste and you spit, then you spout a whole lot of gobbledegook and expect us to swallow it. Body and warmth be damned. You can't take me in that easily.'

'No one was trying to,' said Barker with feeling.

'You've been keen to put one over on us all evening,' replied Hamilton, 'with your "Yes, of course, I'd have known it anywhere" routine. Come on, admit it.'

'I didn't mean to suggest –' added Barker.

'I'll prove it, if you like,' said Hamilton.

The five of us stared at the ungracious guest and, for the first time that evening, I wondered what could possibly be coming next.

'I have heard it said,' continued Hamilton, 'that Sefton Hall boasts one of the finest wine cellars in England. It was laid down by my father and his father before him, though I confess I haven't found the time to continue the tradition.' Barker nodded in belief. 'But my butler knows exactly what I like. I therefore invite you, sir, to join me for lunch on the Saturday after next, when I will produce four wines of the finest vintage for your consideration. And I offer you a wager,' he added, looking straight at Barker. 'Five hundred pounds to fifty a bottle – tempting odds, I'm sure you'll agree – that you will be unable to name any one of them.' He stared belligerently at the distinguished President of the Wine Society.

'The sum is so large that I could not consider –'

'Unwilling to take up the challenge, eh, Barker? Then you are, sir, a coward as well as a humbug.'

After the embarrassing pause that followed, Barker replied, 'As you wish, sir. It appears I am left with no choice but to accept your challenge.'

A satisfied grin appeared on the other man's face. 'You must come along as a witness, Henry,' he said, turning to our host. 'And why don't you bring along that author johnny?' he added, pointing at me. 'Then he'll really have something to write about for a change.'

From Hamilton's manner it was obvious that the feelings of our wives were not to be taken into consideration. Mary gave me a wry smile.

Henry looked anxiously towards me, but I was quite content to be an observer of this unfolding drama. I nodded my assent.

'Good,' said Hamilton, rising from his place, his napkin still tucked under his collar. 'I look forward to seeing the three of you at Sefton Hall on Saturday week. Shall we say twelve thirty?' He bowed to Suzanne.

'I won't be able to join you, I'm afraid,' she said,

clearing up any lingering doubt she might have been included in the invitation. 'I always have lunch with my mother on Saturdays.'

Hamilton waved a hand to signify that it did not concern him one way or the other.

After the strange guest had left we sat in silence for some moments before Henry volunteered a statement. 'I'm sorry about all that,' he began. 'His mother and my aunt are old friends and she's asked me on several occasions to have him over to dinner. It seems no one else will.'

'Don't worry,' said Barker eventually. 'I'll do my best not to let you down. And in return for such excellent hospitality perhaps both of you would be kind enough to leave Saturday evening free? There is,' he explained, 'an inn near Sefton Hall I have wanted to visit for some time: the Hamilton Arms. The food, I'm assured, is more than adequate but the wine list is . . .' he hesitated, 'considered by experts to be exceptional.'

Henry and I both checked our diaries and readily accepted his invitation.

I thought a great deal about Sefton Hamilton during the next ten days and awaited our lunch with a mixture of apprehension and anticipation. On the Saturday morning Henry drove the three of us down to Sefton Park and we arrived a little after twelve thirty. Actually we passed through the massive wrought-iron gates at twelve thirty precisely, but did not reach the front door of the house until twelve thirty-seven.

The great oak door was opened before we had a chance to knock by a tall elegant man in a tail coat, wing collar and black tie. He informed us that he was Adams, the butler. He then escorted us to the morning room, where we were greeted by a large log fire. Above it hung a picture of a disapproving man who I presumed was Sefton Hamilton's grandfather. On the other walls was a massive tapestry of the Battle of Waterloo and an enormous oil of the Crimean War. Antique furniture littered the room and the one sculpture on display was of a Greek figure throwing a discus. Looking around, I reflected that only the telephone belonged to the present century.

Sefton Hamilton entered the room as a gale might hit an unhappy seaside town. Immediately he stood with his back to the fire, blocking any heat we might have been appreciating.

'Whisky!' he bellowed as Adams appeared once again. 'Barker?'

'Not for me,' said Barker with a thin smile.

'Ah,' said Hamilton. 'Want to keep your taste buds at their most sensitive, eh?'

Barker did not reply. Before we went into lunch we learned that the estate was seven thousand acres in size and had some of the finest shooting outside of Scotland. The Hall had one hundred and twelve rooms, one or two of which Hamilton had not visited since he was a child. The roof itself, he assured us finally, was an acre and a half, a statistic that will long remain in my memory as it is the same size as my garden.

The longcase clock in the corner of the room struck one. 'Time for the contest to begin,' declared Hamilton, and marched out of the room like a general who assumes his troops will follow him without question. We did, all the way down thirty yards of corridor to the dining room. The four of us then took our places around a seventeenth-century oak table that could comfortably have seated twenty.

Adorning the centre of the table were two Georgian decanters and two unlabelled bottles. The first bottle was filled with a clear white wine, the first decanter with a red, the second bottle with a richer white and the second decanter with a tawny red substance. In front of the four wines were four white cards. By each lay a slim bundle of fifty-pound notes.

Hamilton took his place in the large chair at the top of the table while Barker and I sat opposite each other in the centre, facing the wine, leaving Henry to occupy the final place at the far end of the table.

The butler stood one pace behind his master's chair. He nodded and four footmen appeared, bearing the first course. A fish and prawn terrine was placed in front of each of us. Adams received a nod from his master before he picked up the first bottle and began to fill Barker's glass. Barker waited for the butler to go round the table and fill the other three glasses before he began his ritual.

First he swirled the wine round while at the same time studying it carefully. Then he sniffed it. He hesitated and a surprised look came over his face. He took a sip.

'Um,' he said eventually. 'I confess, quite a challenge.' He sniffed it again just to be sure. Then he looked up and gave a smile of satisfaction. Hamilton stared at him, his mouth slightly open, although he remained unusually silent.

Barker took one more sip. 'Montagny Tête de Cuvée 1985,' he declared with the confidence of an expert, 'bottled by Louis Latour.' We all looked towards Hamilton who, in contrast, displayed an unhappy frown.

'You're right,' said Hamilton. 'It was bottled by Latour. But that's about as clever as telling us that Heinz bottle tomato sauce. And as my father died in 1984 I can assure you, sir, you are mistaken.' He looked round at his butler to confirm the statement. Adams's face remained inscrutable. Barker turned over the card. It read: 'Chevalier Montrachet Les Demorselles 1983'. He stared at the card, obviously unable to believe his eyes.

'One down and three to go,' Hamilton declared, oblivious to Barker's reaction. The footmen reappeared and took away the fish plates, to replace them a few moments later with lightly cooked grouse. While its accompaniments were being served Barker did not speak. He just stared at the other three decanters, not even hearing his host inform Henry who his guests were to be for the first shoot of the season the following week. I remember that the names corresponded roughly with the ones Hamilton had suggested for his ideal Cabinet.

Barker nibbled at the grouse as he waited for Adams to fill a glass from the first decanter. He had not finished his terrine after the opening failure, only taking the occasional sip of water.

'As Adams and I spent a considerable part of our morning selecting the wines for this little challenge, let us hope you can do better this time,' said Hamilton, unable to hide his satisfaction. Barker once again began to swirl the wine round. He seemed to take longer this time, sniffing it several times before putting his glass to his lips and finally sipping from it.

A smile of instant recognition appeared on his face and he did not hesitate. 'Château la Louvière 1978.'

'This time you have the correct year, sir, but you have insulted the wine.'

Immediately Barker turned the card over and read it out incredulously: Château Lafite 1978. Even I knew that to be one of the finest clarets one might ever hope to taste. Barker lapsed into a deep silence and continued to nibble at his food. Hamilton appeared to be enjoying the wine almost as much as the half-time score. 'One hundred pounds to me, nothing to the President of the Wine Society,' he reminded us. Embarrassed, Henry and I tried to keep the conversation going until the third course had been served – a lemon and lime soufflé which could not compare in presentation or subtlety with any of Suzanne's offerings.

'Shall we move on to my third challenge?' asked Hamilton crisply.

Once again, Adams picked up a decanter and began to pour the wine. I was surprised to see that he spilled a little as he filled Barker's glass.

'Clumsy oaf,' barked Hamilton.

'I do apologise, sir,' said Adams. He removed the spilled drop from the wooden table with a napkin. As he did so he stared at Barker with a desperate look that I felt sure had nothing to do with the spilling of the wine. However, he remained mute as he continued to circle the table.

Once again Barker went through his ritual, the swirling, the sniffing and finally the tasting. This time he took even longer. Hamilton became impatient and drummed the great Jacobean table with his podgy fingers.

'It's a Sauternes,' began Barker.

'Any half-wit could tell you that,' said Hamilton. 'I want to know the year and the vintage.'

His guest hesitated.

'Château Guiraud 1976,' he said flatly.

'At least you are consistent,' said Hamilton. 'You're always wrong.'

Barker flicked over the card.

'Château d'Yquem 1980,' he said in disbelief. It was a vintage that I had only seen at the bottom of wine lists in expensive restaurants and had never had the privilege of tasting. It puzzled me greatly that Barker could have been wrong about the Mona Lisa of wines.

Barker quickly turned towards Hamilton to protest and must have seen Adams standing behind his master, all six foot three of the man trembling, at exactly the same time I did. I wanted Hamilton to leave the room so I could ask Adams what was making him so fearful, but the owner of Sefton Hall was now in full cry.

Meanwhile Barker gazed at the butler for a moment more and, sensing his discomfort, lowered his eyes and contributed nothing else to the conversation until the port was poured some twenty minutes later.

'Your last chance to avoid complete humiliation,' said Hamilton.

A cheese board, displaying several varieties, was brought round and each guest selected his choice – I stuck to a Cheddar that I could have told Hamilton had not been made in Somerset. Meanwhile the port was poured by the butler, who was now as white as a sheet. I began to wonder if he was going to faint, but somehow he managed to fill all four glasses before returning to stand a pace behind his master's chair. Hamilton noticed nothing untoward.

Barker drank the port, not bothering with any of his previous preliminaries.

'Taylors,' he began.

'Agreed,' said Hamilton. 'But as there are only

three decent suppliers of port in the world, the year can be all that matters – as you, in your exalted position, must be well aware, Mr Barker.'

Freddie nodded his agreement. 'Nineteen seventy-five,' he said firmly, then quickly flicked the card over.

'Taylors 1927', I read upside-down.

Once again Barker turned sharply towards his host, who was rocking with laughter. The butler stared back at his master's guest with haunted eyes. Barker hesitated only for a moment before removing a cheque book from his inside pocket. He filled in the name 'Sefton Hamilton' and the figure of £200. He signed it and wordlessly passed the cheque along the table to his host.

'That was only half the bargain,' said Hamilton, enjoying every moment of his triumph.

Barker rose, paused and said, 'I am a humbug.'

'You are indeed, sir,' said Hamilton.

After spending three of the most unpleasant hours of my life, I managed to escape with Henry and Freddie Barker a little after four o'clock. As Henry drove away from Sefton Hall neither of us uttered a word. Perhaps we both felt that Barker should be allowed the first comment.

'I fear, gentlemen,' he said eventually, 'I shall not be good company for the next few hours, and so I will, with your permission, take a brisk walk and join you both for dinner at the Hamilton Arms around seven thirty. I have booked a table for eight o'clock.' Without another word, Barker signalled that Henry should bring the car to a halt and we watched as he climbed out and headed off down a country lane. Henry did not drive on until his friend was well out of sight.

My sympathies were entirely with Barker, although I remained puzzled by the whole affair. How could the President of the Wine Society make such basic mistakes? After all, I could read one page of Dickens and know it wasn't Graham Greene.

Like Dr Watson, I felt I required a fuller explanation.

Barker found us sitting round the fire in the private bar at the Hamilton Arms a little after seven thirty that night. Following his exercise, he appeared in far better spirits. He chatted about nothing consequential and didn't once mention what had taken place at lunchtime.

It must have been a few minutes later, when I turned to check the old clock above the door, that I saw Hamilton's butler seated at the bar in earnest conversation with the innkeeper. I would have thought nothing of it had I not noticed the same terrified look that I had witnessed earlier in the afternoon as he pointed in our direction. The innkeeper appeared equally anxious, as if he had been found guilty of serving half-measures by a customs and excise officer.

He picked up some menus and walked over to our table.

'We've no need for those,' said Barker. 'Your reputation goes before you. We are in your hands. Whatever you suggest we will happily consume.'

'Thank you, sir,' he said and passed our host the wine list.

Barker studied the contents inside the leather-bound covers for some time before a large smile appeared on his face. 'I think you had better select the wines as well,' he said, 'as I have a feeling you know the sort of thing I would expect.'

'Of course, sir,' said the innkeeper as Freddie passed back the wine list leaving me totally mystified, remembering that this was Barker's first visit to the inn.

The innkeeper left for the kitchens while we chatted away and didn't reappear for some fifteen minutes.

'Your table is ready, gentlemen,' he said, and we followed him into an adjoining dining room. There were only a dozen tables but as ours was the last to be filled there was no doubting the inn's popularity.

The innkeeper had selected a light supper of consommé, followed by thin slices of duck, almost as if he had known that we would be unable to handle another heavy meal after our lunch at the Hall.

I was also surprised to find that all the wines he had chosen were served in decanters and I assumed that the innkeeper must therefore have selected the house wines. As each was poured and consumed I admit that, to my untutored palate, they seemed far superior to those which I had drunk at Sefton Hall earlier that day. Barker certainly seemed to linger over every mouthful and on one occasion said appreciatively, 'This is the real McCoy.'

At the end of the evening when our table had been cleared we sat back and enjoyed a magnificent port and smoked cigars.

It was at this point that Henry mentioned Hamilton for the first time.

'Are you going to let us into the mystery of what really happened at lunch today?' he asked.

'I'm still not altogether sure myself,' came back Barker's reply, 'but I am certain of one thing: Mr Hamilton's father was a man who knew his wines, while his son doesn't.'

I would have pressed Barker further on the subject if the innkeeper had not arrived by his side at that moment.

'An excellent meal,' Barker declared. 'And as for the wine – quite exceptional.'

'You are kind, sir,' said the innkeeper, as he handed him the bill.

My curiosity got the better of me, I'm sorry to admit, and I glanced at the bottom of the slim strip of paper. I couldn't believe my eyes – the bill came to two hundred pounds.

To my surprise, Barker only commented, 'Very reasonable, considering.' He wrote out a cheque and passed it over to the innkeeper. 'I have only tasted Château d'Yquem 1980 once before today,' he added, 'and Taylors 1927 never.'

The innkeeper smiled. 'I hope you enjoyed them both, sir. I feel sure you wouldn't have wanted to see them wasted on a humbug.'

Barker nodded his agreement.

I watched as the innkeeper left the dining room and returned to his place behind the bar.

He passed the cheque over to Adams the butler, who studied it for a moment, smiled and then tore it into little pieces.

A CHAPTER OF
ACCIDENTS

WE FIRST MET Patrick Travers on our annual winter holiday to Verbier. We were waiting at the ski lift that first Saturday morning when a man who must have been in his early forties stood aside to allow Caroline to take his place, so that we could travel up together. He explained that he had already completed two runs that morning and didn't mind waiting. I thanked him and thought nothing more of it.

As soon as we reach the top my wife and I always go our separate ways, she to the A-slope to join Marcel, who only instructs advanced skiers – she has been skiing since the age of seven – I to the B-slope and any instructor who is available – I took up skiing at the age of forty-one – and frankly the B-slope is still too advanced for me though I don't dare admit as much, especially to Caroline. We always meet up again at the ski lift after completing our different runs.

That evening we bumped into Travers at the hotel bar. Since he seemed to be on his own we invited him to join us for dinner. He proved to be an amusing companion and we passed a pleasant enough evening together. He flirted politely with my wife without ever overstepping the mark and she appeared to be flattered by his attentions. Over the years I have become used to men being attracted to Caroline and I never need reminding how lucky I am. During dinner we learned that Travers was a merchant banker with an office in the City and a flat in Eaton Square. He had come to Verbier every year since he had been taken on a school trip in the late Fifties, he told us. He still prided himself on being the first on the ski lift every morning, almost always beating the local blades up and down.

Travers appeared to be genuinely interested in the fact that I ran a small West End art gallery; as it turned out, he was something of a collector himself, specialising in minor Impressionists. He promised he would drop by and see my next exhibition when he was back in London.

I assured him that he would be most welcome but never gave it a second thought. In fact I only saw Travers a couple of times over the rest of the holiday, once talking to the wife of a friend of mine who owned a gallery that specialises in oriental rugs, and later I noticed him following Caroline expertly down the treacherous A-slope.

It was six weeks later, and some minutes before I could place him that night at my gallery. I had to rack that part of one's memory which recalls names, a skill politicians rely on every day.

'Good to see you, Edward,' he said. 'I saw the write-up you got in the *Independent* and remembered your kind invitation to the private view.'

'Glad you could make it, Patrick,' I replied, remembering just in time.

'I'm not a champagne man myself,' he told me, 'but I'll travel a long way to see a Vuillard.'

'You think highly of him?'

'Oh yes. I would compare him favourably with Pissarro and Bonnard, and he still remains one of the most underrated of the Impressionists.'

'I agree,' I replied. 'But my gallery has felt that way about Vuillard for some considerable time.'

'How much is "The Lady at the Window"?' he asked.

'Eighty thousand pounds,' I said quietly.

'It reminds me of a picture of his in the Metropolitan,' he said, as he studied the reproduction in the catalogue.

I was impressed, and told Travers that the Vuillard in New York had been painted within a month of the one he so admired.

He nodded. 'And the small nude?'

'Forty-seven thousand,' I told him.

'Mrs Hensell, the wife of his dealer and Vuillard's second mistress, if I'm not mistaken. The French are always so much more civilised about these things than we are. But my favourite painting in this exhibition,' he continued, 'compares surely with the finest of his work.' He turned to face the large oil of a young girl playing a piano, her mother bending to turn a page of the score.

'Magnificent,' he said. 'Dare I ask how much?'

'Three hundred and seventy thousand pounds,' I said, wondering if such a price tag put it out of Travers's bracket.

'What a super party, Edward,' said a voice from behind my shoulder.

'Percy!' I cried, turning round. 'I thought you said you wouldn't be able to make it.'

'Yes I did, old fellow, but I decided I couldn't sit at home alone all the time, so I've come to drown my sorrows in champagne.'

'Quite right too,' I said. 'Sorry to hear about Diana,' I added as Percy moved on. When I turned back to continue my conversation with Patrick Travers he was nowhere to be seen. I searched around the room and spotted him standing in the far corner of the gallery chatting to my wife, a glass of champagne in his hand. She was wearing an off-the-shoulder green dress that I considered a little too modern. Travers's eyes seemed to be glued to a spot a few inches below the shoulders. I would have thought nothing of it had he spoken to anyone else that evening.

The next occasion on which I saw Travers was about a week later on returning from the bank with some petty cash. Once again he was standing in front of the Vuillard oil of mother and daughter at the piano.

'Good morning, Patrick,' I said as I joined him.

'I can't seem to get that picture out of my mind,' he declared, as he continued to stare at the two figures.

'Understandably.'

'I don't suppose you would allow me to live with them for a week or two until I can finally make up my mind? Naturally I would be quite happy to leave a deposit.'

'Of course,' I said. 'I would require a bank reference as well and the deposit would be twenty-five thousand pounds.'

He agreed to both requests without hesitation so I asked him where he would like the picture delivered. He handed me a card which revealed his address in Eaton Square. The following morning his bankers confirmed that three hundred and seventy thousand pounds would not be a problem for their client.

Within twenty-four hours the Vuillard had been taken round to his home and hung in the dining room on the ground floor. He phoned back in the afternoon to thank me and asked if Caroline and I would care to join him for dinner; he wanted, he said, a second opinion on how the painting looked.

With three hundred and seventy thousand pounds at stake I didn't feel it was an invitation I could reasonably turn down, and in any case Caroline seemed eager to accept, explaining that she was interested to see what his house was like.

We dined with Travers the following Thursday.

We turned out to be the only guests, and I remember being surprised that there wasn't a Mrs Travers or at least a resident girlfriend. He was a thoughtful host and the meal he had arranged was superb. However, I considered at the time that he seemed a little too solicitous with Caroline, although she certainly gave the impression of enjoying his undivided attention. At one point I began to wonder if either of them would have noticed if I had disappeared into thin air.

When we left Eaton Square that night Travers told me that he had almost made up his mind about the picture, which made me feel the evening had served at least some purpose.

Six days later the painting was returned to the gallery with a note attached explaining that he no longer cared for it. Travers did not elaborate on his reasons, but simply ended by saying that he hoped to drop by some time and reconsider the other Vuillards. Disappointed, I returned his deposit, but realised that customers often do come back, sometimes months, even years later.

But Travers never did.

It was about a month later that I learned why he would never return. I was lunching at the large centre table at my club, as in most all-male establishments the table reserved for members who drift in on their own. Percy Fellows was the next to enter the dining room so he took a seat opposite me. I hadn't seen him to talk to since the private view of the Vuillard exhibition and we hadn't really had much of a conversation then. Percy was one of the most respected antique dealers in England and I had once even done a successful barter with him, a Charles II writing desk in exchange for a Dutch landscape by Utrillo.

I repeated how sorry I was to learn about Diana.

'It was always going to end in divorce,' he explained. 'She was in and out of every bedroom in London. I was beginning to look a complete cuckold, and that bloody man Travers was the last straw.'

'Travers?' I said, not understanding.

'Patrick Travers, the man named in my divorce petition. Ever come across him?'

'I know the name,' I said hesitantly, wanting to hear more before I admitted to our slight acquaintanceship.

'Funny,' he said. 'Could have sworn I saw him at the private view.'

'But what do you mean, he was the last straw?' I asked, trying to take his mind off the opening.

'Met the bloody fellow at Ascot, didn't we? Joined us for lunch, happily drank my champagne, ate my strawberries and cream and then before the week was out had bedded my wife. But that's not the half of it.'

'The half of it?'

'The man had the nerve to come round to my shop and put down a large deposit on a Georgian table. Then he invites the two of us round to dinner to see how it looks. After he's had enough time to make love to Diana he returns them both slightly soiled. You don't look too well, old fellow,' said Percy suddenly. 'Something wrong with the food? Never been the same since Harry left for the Carlton. I've written to the wine committee about it several times but –'

'No, I'm fine,' I said. 'I just need a little fresh air. Please excuse me, Percy.'

It was on the walk back from my club that I decided I would have to do something about Mr Travers.

The next morning I waited for the mail to arrive and checked any envelopes addressed to Caroline. Nothing seemed untoward but then I decided that Travers wouldn't have been foolish enough to commit anything to paper. I also began to eavesdrop on her telephone conversations, but he was not among the callers, at least not while I was at home. I even checked the mileometer on her Mini to see if she had driven any long distances, but then Eaton Square isn't all that far. It's often what you don't do that gives the game away, I decided: we didn't make love for a fortnight, and she didn't comment.

I continued to watch Caroline more carefully over the next fortnight but it became obvious to me that Travers must have tired of her about the same time as he had returned the Vuillard. This only made me more angry.

I then formed a plan of revenge that seemed quite extraordinary to me at the time and I assumed that in a matter of days I would get over it, even forget it. But I didn't. If anything, the idea grew into an obsession. I began to convince myself that it was my bounden duty to do away with Travers before he besmirched any more of my friends.

I have never in my life knowingly broken the law. Parking fines annoy me, dropped litter offends me and I pay my VAT on the same day the frightful buff envelope drops through the letterbox.

Nevertheless once I'd decided what had to be done I set about my task meticulously. At first I had considered shooting Travers until I discovered how hard it is to get a gun licence and that if I did the job properly, he would end up feeling very little pain, which wasn't what I had planned for him; then poisoning crossed my mind – but that requires a witnessed prescription and I still wouldn't be able to watch the long slow death I desired. Then strangling, which I decided would necessitate too much courage – and in any case he was a bigger man than me so *I* might end up being the one who was strangled. Then drowning, which could take years to get the man near any water and then I might not be able to hang around to make sure he went under for the third time. I even gave some thought to running over the damned man, but dropped that idea when I realised opportunity would be almost nil and besides, I wouldn't be left any time to check if he was dead. I was quickly becoming aware just how hard it is to kill someone – and get away with it.

I sat awake at night reading the biographies of murderers, but as they had all been caught and found guilty that didn't fill me with much confidence. I turned to detective novels which always seemed to allow for a degree of coincidence, luck and surprise that I was unwilling to risk, until I came across a rewarding line from Conan Doyle: 'Any intended victim who has a regular routine immediately makes himself more vulnerable'. And then I recalled one routine of which Travers was particularly proud. It required a further six-month wait on my part but that also gave me more time to perfect my plan. I used the enforced wait well because whenever Caroline was away for more than twenty-four hours, I booked in for a skiing lesson on the dry slope at Harrow.

I found it surprisingly easy to discover when Travers would be returning to Verbier, and I was able to organise the winter holiday so that our paths would cross for only three days, a period of time quite sufficient for me to commit my first crime.

Caroline and I arrived in Verbier on the second Friday in January. She had commented on the state of my nerves more than once over the Christmas period, and hoped the holiday would help me relax. I could hardly explain to her that it was the thought of the holiday that was making me so tense. It didn't help when she asked me on the plane to Switzerland if I thought Travers might be there this year.

On the first morning after our arrival we took the ski lift up at about ten thirty and, once we had reached the top, Caroline duly reported to Marcel. As she departed with him for the A-slope I returned to the B-slope to work on my own. As always we agreed to meet back at the ski lift or, if we missed each other, at least for lunch.

During the days that followed I went over and over the plan I had perfected in my mind and practised so diligently at Harrow until I felt sure it was foolproof. By the end of the first week I had convinced myself I was ready.

The night before Travers was due to arrive I was the last to leave the slopes. Even Caroline commented on how much my skiing had improved and she suggested to Marcel that I was ready for the A-slope with its sharper bends and steeper inclines.

'Next year, perhaps,' I told her, trying to make light of it, and returned to the B-slope.

During the final morning I skied over the first mile of the course again and again, and became so preoccupied with my work that I quite forgot to join Caroline for lunch.

In the afternoon I checked and rechecked the placing of every red flag marking the run, and once I was convinced the last skier had left the slope for the evening I collected about thirty of the flags and replaced them at intervals I had carefully worked out.

My final task was to check the prepared patch before building a large mound of snow some twenty paces above the chosen spot. Once my preparations were complete I skied slowly down the mountain in the fading light.

'Are you trying to win an Olympic gold medal or something?' Caroline asked me when I eventually got back to our room. I closed the bathroom door so she couldn't expect a reply.

Travers checked in to the hotel an hour later.

I waited until the early evening before I joined him at the bar for a drink. He seemed a little nervous when he first saw me, but I quickly put him at ease. His old self-confidence soon returned, which only made me more determined to carry out my plan. I left him at the bar a few minutes before Caroline came down for dinner so that she would not see the two of us together. Innocent surprise would be necessary once the deed had been done.

'Unlike you to eat so little, especially as you missed your lunch,' Caroline commented as we left the dining room that night.

I made no comment as we passed Travers seated at the bar, his hand on the knee of another innocent middle-aged woman.

I did not sleep for one second that night and I crept out of bed just before six the next morning, careful not to wake Caroline. Everything was laid out on the bathroom floor just as I had left it the night before. A few moments later I was dressed and ready.

I walked down the back stairs of the hotel, avoiding the lift, and crept out by the 'fire exit', realising for the first time what a thief must feel like. I had a woollen cap pulled well down over my ears and a pair of snow goggles covering my eyes: not even Caroline would have recognised me.

I arrived at the bottom of the ski lift forty minutes before it was due to open. As I stood alone behind the little shed that housed the electrical machinery to work the lift I realised that everything now depended on Travers's sticking to his routine. I wasn't sure I could go through with it if my plan had to be moved on to the following day. As I waited, I stamped my feet in the freshly fallen snow, and slapped my arms around my chest to keep warm. Every few moments I kept peering round the corner of the building in the hope that I would see him striding towards me. At last a speck appeared at the bottom of the hill by the side of the road, a pair of skis resting on the man's shoulders. But what if it didn't turn out to be Travers?

I stepped out from behind the shed a few moments later to join the warmly wrapped man. It *was* Travers and he could not hide his surprise at seeing me standing there. I started up a casual conversation about being unable to sleep, and how I thought I might as well put in a few runs before the rush began. Now all I needed was the ski lift to start up on time. A few minutes after seven an engineer arrived and the vast oily mechanism cranked into action.

We were the first two to take our places on those

little seats before heading up and over the deep ravine. I kept turning back to check there was still no one else in sight.

'I usually manage to complete a full run even before the second person arrives,' Travers told me when the lift had reached its highest point. I looked back again to be sure we were now well out of sight of the engineer working the lift, then peered down some two hundred feet and wondered what it would be like to land head first in the ravine. I began to feel dizzy and wished I hadn't looked down.

The ski lift jerked slowly on up the icy wire until we finally reached the landing point.

'Damn,' I said, as we jumped off our little seats. 'Marcel isn't here.'

'Never is at this time,' said Travers, making off towards the advanced slope. 'Far too early for him.'

'I don't suppose you would come down with me?' I said, calling after Travers.

He stopped and looked back suspiciously.

'Caroline thinks I'm ready to join you,' I explained, 'but I'm not so sure and would value a second opinion. I've broken my own record for the B-slope several times, but I wouldn't want to make a fool of myself in front of my wife.'

'Well, I –'

'I'd ask Marcel if he were here. And in any case you're the best skier I know.'

'Well, if you –' he began.

'Just the once, then you can spend the rest of your holiday on the A-slope. You could even treat the run as a warm-up.'

'Might make a change, I suppose,' he said.

'Just the once,' I repeated. 'That's all I'll need. Then you'll be able to tell me if I'm good enough.'

'Shall we make a race of it?' he said, taking me by surprise just as I began clamping on my skis. I couldn't complain; all the books on murder had warned me to be prepared for the unexpected. 'That's one way we can find out if you're ready,' he added cockily.

'If you insist. Don't forget, I'm older and less experienced than you,' I reminded him. I checked my skis quickly because I knew I had to start off in front of him.

'But you know the B-course backwards,' he retorted. 'I've never even seen it before.'

'I'll agree to a race, but only if you'll consider a wager,' I replied.

For the first time I could see I had caught his interest. 'How much?' he asked.

'Oh, nothing so vulgar as money,' I said. 'The winner gets to tell Caroline the truth.'

'The truth?' he said, looking puzzled.

'Yes,' I replied, and shot off down the hill before he could respond. I got a good start as I skied in and out of the red flags, but looking back over my shoulder I could see he had recovered quickly and was already chasing hard after me. I realised that it was vital for me to stay in front of him for the first third of the course, but I could already feel him cutting down my lead.

After half a mile of swerving and driving he shouted, 'You'll have to go a lot faster than that if you hope to beat me.' His arrogant boast only pushed me to stay ahead but I kept the lead only because of my advantage of knowing every twist and turn during that first mile. Once I was sure that I would reach the vital newly marked route before he could I began to relax. After all, I had practised over the next two hundred metres fifty times a day for the last ten days, but I was only too aware that this time was the only one that mattered.

I glanced over my shoulder to see he was now about thirty metres behind me. I began to slow slightly as we approached the prepared ice patch, hoping he wouldn't notice or would think I'd lost my nerve. I held back even more when I reached the top of the patch until I could almost feel the sound of his breathing. Then, quite suddenly, the moment before I would have hit the ice I ploughed my skis and came to a complete halt in the mound of snow I had built the previous night. Travers sailed past me at about forty miles an hour, and seconds later flew high into the air over the ravine with a scream I will never forget. I couldn't get myself to look over the edge as I knew he must have broken every bone in his body the moment he hit the snow some hundred feet below.

I carefully levelled the mound of snow that had

saved my life and then clambered back up the mountain as fast as I could go, gathering the thirty flags that had heralded my false route. Then I skied from side to side replacing them in their correct positions on the B-slope, some one hundred metres above my carefully prepared ice patch. Once each one was back in place I skied on down the hill, feeling like an Olympic champion. When I reached the base of the slope I pulled up my hood to cover my head and didn't remove my snow goggles. I unstrapped my skis and walked casually towards the hotel. I re-entered the building by the rear door and was back in bed by seven forty.

I tried to control my breathing but it was some time before my pulse had returned to normal. Caroline woke a few minutes later, turned over and put her arms round me.

'Ugh,' she said, 'you're frozen. Have you been sleeping without the covers on?'

I laughed. 'You must have pulled them off during the night.'

'Go and have a hot bath.'

After I had had a quick bath we made love and I dressed a second time, double-checking that I had left no clues of my early flight before going down to breakfast.

As Caroline was pouring my second cup of coffee, I heard the ambulance siren at first coming from the town and then later returning.

'Hope it wasn't a bad accident,' my wife said, as she continued to pour her coffee.

'What?' I said, a little too loudly, glancing up from the previous day's *Times*.

'The siren, silly. There must have been an accident on the mountain. Probably Travers,' she said.

'Travers?' I said, even more loudly.

'Patrick Travers. I saw him at the bar last night. I didn't mention it to you because I know you don't care for him.'

'But why Travers?' I asked nervously.

'Doesn't he always claim he's the first on the slope every morning? Even beats the instructors up to the top.'

'Does he?' I said.

'You must remember. We were going up for the first time the day we met him when he was already on his third run.'

'Was he?'

'You are being dim this morning, Edward. Did you get out of bed the wrong side?' she asked, laughing.

I didn't reply

'Well, I only hope it *is* Travers,' Caroline added, sipping her coffee. 'I never did like the man.'

'Why not?' I asked, somewhat taken aback.

'He once made a pass at me,' she said casually.

I stared across at her, unable to speak.

'Aren't you going to ask what happened?'

'I'm so stunned I don't know what to say,' I replied.

'He was all over me at the gallery that night and then invited me out to lunch after we had dinner with him. I told him to get lost,' Caroline said. She touched me gently on the hand. 'I've never mentioned it to you before because I thought it might have been the reason he returned the Vuillard, and that only made me feel guilty.'

'But it's me who should feel guilty,' I said, fumbling with a piece of toast.

'Oh, no, darling, you're not guilty of anything. In any case, if I ever decided to be unfaithful it wouldn't be with a lounge lizard like that. Good heavens no. Diana had already warned me what to expect from him. Not my style at all.'

I sat there thinking of Travers on his way to a morgue, or even worse, still buried under the snow, knowing there was nothing I could do about it.

'You know, I think the time really has come for you to tackle the A-slope,' Caroline said as we finished breakfast. 'Your skiing has improved beyond words.'

'Yes,' I replied, more than a little preoccupied.

I hardly spoke another word as we made our way together to the foot of the mountain.

'Are you all right, darling?' Caroline asked as we travelled up side by side on the lift.

'Fine,' I said, unable to look down into the ravine as we reached the highest point. Was Travers still down there, or already in the morgue?

'Stop looking like a frightened child. After all the work you've put in this week you're more than ready to join me,' she said reassuringly.

I smiled weakly. When we reached the top, I

jumped off the ski lift just a moment too early, and knew immediately I took my second step that I had sprained an ankle.

I received no sympathy from Caroline. She was convinced I was putting it on in order to avoid attempting the advanced run. She swept past me and sped on down the mountain while I returned in ignominy via the lift. When I reached the bottom I glanced towards the engineer but he didn't give me a second look. I hobbled over to the First Aid post and checked in. Caroline joined me a few minutes later.

I explained to her that the duty orderly thought it might be a fracture and it had been suggested I report to the hospital immediately.

Caroline frowned, removed her skis and went off to find a taxi to take us to the hospital. It wasn't a long journey but it was one the taxi driver evidently had done many times before from the way he took the slippery bends.

'I ought to be able to dine out on this for about a year,' Caroline promised me as we entered the double doors of the hospital.

'Would you be kind enough to wait outside, madam?' asked a male orderly as I was ushered into the X-ray room.

'Yes, but will I ever see my poor husband again?' she mocked as the door was closed in front of her.

I entered a room full of sophisticated machinery presided over by an expensively dressed doctor. I told him what I thought was wrong with me and he lifted the offending foot gently up on to an X-ray machine. Moments later he was studying the large negative.

'There's no fracture there,' he assured me, pointing to the bone. 'But if you are still in any pain it might be wise for me to bind the ankle up tightly.' The doctor then pinned my X-ray next to five others hanging from a rail.

'Am I the sixth person already today?' I asked, looking up at the row of X-rays.

'No, no,' he said, laughing. 'The other five are all the same man. I think he must have tried to fly over the ravine, the fool.'

'Over the ravine?'

'Yes, showing off, I suspect,' he said as he began to bind my ankle. 'We get one every year but this poor fellow broke both his legs and an arm, and will have a nasty scar on his face to remind him of his stupidity. Lucky to be alive in my opinion.'

'Lucky to be alive?' I repeated weakly.

'Yes, but only because he didn't know what he was doing. My fourteen-year-old skis over that ravine and can land like a seagull on water. He, on the other hand,' the doctor pointed to the X-rays, 'won't be skiing again this holiday. In fact, he won't be walking for at least six months.'

'Really?' I said.

'And as for you,' he added, after he finished binding me up, 'just rest the ankle in ice every three hours and change the bandage once a day. You should be back on the slopes again in a couple of days, three at the most.'

'We're flying back this evening,' I told him as I gingerly got to my feet.

'Good timing,' he said, smiling.

I hobbled happily out of the X-ray room to find Caroline head down in *Elle*.

'You look pleased with yourself,' she said, looking up.

'I am. It turns out to be nothing worse than two broken legs, a broken arm and a scar on the face.'

'How stupid of me,' said Caroline, 'I thought it was a simple sprain.'

'Not me,' I told her. 'Travers – the accident this morning, you remember? The ambulance. Still, they assure me he'll live,' I added.

'Pity,' she said, linking her arm through mine. 'After all the trouble you took, I was rather hoping you'd succeed.'

THE LOOPHOLE

'THAT ISN'T the version I heard,' said Philip.

One of the club members seated at the bar glanced round at the sound of raised voices, but when he saw who was involved only smiled and continued his conversation.

The Haslemere Golf Club was fairly crowded that Saturday morning. And just before lunch it was often difficult to find a seat in the spacious clubhouse.

Two of the members had already ordered their second round and settled themselves in the alcove overlooking the first hole long before the room began to fill up. Philip Masters and Michael Gilmour had finished their Saturday morning game earlier than usual and now seemed engrossed in conversation.

'And what did you hear?' asked Michael Gilmour quietly, but in a voice that carried.

'That you weren't altogether blameless in the matter.'

'I most certainly was,' said Michael. 'What are you suggesting?'

'I'm not suggesting anything,' said Philip. 'But don't forget, you can't fool me. I employed you myself

239

once and I've known you for far too long to accept everything you say at face value.'

'I wasn't trying to fool anyone,' said Michael. 'It's common knowledge that I lost my job. I've never suggested otherwise.'

'Agreed. But what isn't common knowledge is *how* you lost your job and why you haven't been able to find a new one.'

'I haven't been able to find a new one for the simple reason jobs aren't that easy to come by at the moment. And by the way, it's not my fault you're a success story and a bloody millionaire.'

'And it's not my fault that you're penniless and always out of work. The truth is that jobs are easy enough to come by for someone who can supply references from his last employer.'

'Just what are you hinting at?' said Michael.

'I'm not hinting at anything.'

Several members had stopped taking part in the conversation in front of them as they tried to listen to the one going on behind them.

'What I am saying,' Philip continued, 'is that no one will employ you for the simple reason that you can't find anyone who will supply you with a reference – and everybody knows it.'

Everybody didn't know it, which explained why most people in the room were now trying to find out.

'I was made redundant,' insisted Michael.

The Loophole

'In your case redundant was just a euphemism for sacked. No one pretended otherwise at the time.'

'I was made redundant,' repeated Michael, 'for the simple reason that the company profits turned out to be a little disappointing this year.'

'A little disappointing? That's rich. They were non-existent.'

'Simply because we lost one or two of our major accounts to rivals.'

'Rivals who, I'm informed, were only too happy to pay for a little inside information.'

By now most members of the club had cut short their own conversations as they leaned, twisted, turned and bent in an effort to capture every word coming from the two men seated in the window alcove of the club room.

'The loss of those accounts was fully explained in the report to shareholders at this year's AGM,' said Michael.

'But was it explained to those same shareholders how a former employee could afford to buy a new car only a matter of days after being sacked?' pursued Philip. 'A second car, I might add.' Philip took a sip of his tomato juice.

'It wasn't a new car,' said Michael defensively. 'It was a second-hand Mini and I bought it with part of my redundancy pay when I had to return the company car. And in any case, you know Carol needs her own car for the job at the bank.

'Frankly, I am amazed Carol has stuck it for so long as she has after all you've put her through.'

'All I've put her through; what are you implying?' asked Michael.

'I am not *implying* anything,' Philip retorted. 'But the fact is that a certain young woman who shall remain nameless' – this piece of information seemed to disappoint most eavesdroppers – 'also became redundant at about the same time, not to mention pregnant.'

The barman had not been asked for a drink for nearly seven minutes, and by now there were few members still affecting not to be listening to the altercation between the two men. Some were even staring in open disbelief.

'But I hardly knew her,' protested Michael.

'As I said, that's not the version I heard. And what's more I'm told the child bears a striking resemblance –'

'That's going too far –'

'Only if you have nothing to hide,' said Philip grimly.

'You know I've nothing to hide.'

'Not even the blonde hairs Carol found all over the back seat of the new Mini. The girl at work was a blonde, wasn't she?'

'Yes, but those hairs came from a golden retriever.'

'You don't have a golden retriever.'

'I know, but the dog belonged to the last owner.'

'That bitch didn't belong to the last owner, and I refuse to believe Carol fell for that old chestnut.'

'She believed it because it was the truth.'

'The truth, I fear, is something you lost contact with a long time ago. You were sacked, first because you couldn't keep your hands off anything in a skirt under forty, and second, because you couldn't keep your fingers out of the till. I ought to know. Don't forget I had to get rid of you for the same reasons.'

Michael jumped up, his cheeks almost the colour of Philip's tomato juice. He raised his clenched fist and was about to take a swing at Philip when Colonel Mather, the club president, appeared at his side.

'Good morning, sir,' said Philip calmly, rising for the Colonel.

'Good morning, Philip,' the Colonel barked. 'Don't you think this little misunderstanding has gone quite far enough?'

'Little misunderstanding?' protested Michael. 'Didn't you hear what he's been saying about me?'

'Every word, unfortunately, like any other member present,' said the Colonel. Turning back to Philip, he added, 'Perhaps you two should shake hands like good fellows and call it a day.'

'Shake hands with that philandering, double-crossing shyster? Never,' said Philip. 'I tell you, Colonel, he's not fit to be a member of this club, and I can assure you that you've only heard half the story.'

Before the Colonel could attempt another round

of diplomacy Michael sprang on Philip and it took three men younger than the club president to prise them apart. The Colonel immediately ordered both men off the premises, warning them that their conduct would be reported to the house committee at its next monthly meeting. And until that meeting had taken place, they were both suspended.

The club secretary, Jeremy Howard, escorted the two men off the premises and watched Philip get into his Rolls-Royce and drive sedately down the drive and out through the gates. He had to wait on the steps of the club for several minutes before Michael departed in his Mini. He appeared to be sitting in the front seat writing something. When he had eventually passed through the club gates, the secretary turned on his heels and made his way back to the bar. What they did to each other after they left the grounds was none of his business.

Back in the clubhouse, the secretary found that the conversation had not returned to the likely winner of the President's Putter, the seeding of the Ladies' Handicap Cup, or who might be prevailed upon to sponsor the Youth Tournament that year.

'They seemed in a jolly enough mood when I passed them on the sixteenth hole earlier this morning,' the club captain informed the Colonel.

The Colonel admitted to being mystified. He had known both men since the day they joined the club nearly fifteen years before. They weren't bad lads, he assured the captain; in fact he rather liked them. They had played a round of golf every Saturday morning for as long as anyone could remember, and never a cross word had been known to pass between them.

'Pity,' said the Colonel. 'I was hoping to ask Masters to sponsor the Youth Tournament this year.'

'Good idea, but I can't see you pulling that off now.'

'I can't imagine what they thought they were up to.'

'Can it simply be that Philip is such a success story and Michael has fallen on hard times?' suggested the captain.

'No, there's more to it than that,' replied the Colonel. 'This morning's little episode requires a fuller explanation,' he added sagely.

Everyone in the club was aware that Philip Masters had built up his own business from scratch after he had left his first job as a kitchen salesman. 'Ready-Fit Kitchens' had started in a shed at the end of Philip's garden and ended up in a factory on the other side of town which employed over three hundred people. After Ready-Fit went public the financial press speculated that Philip's shares alone had to be worth a couple of million. When five years later the company was taken over by the John Lewis Partnership, it became public knowledge that Philip had walked away from the deal with a cheque for seventeen million pounds and a five-year service contract that would have pleased a pop star. Some of the windfall had been spent on a magnificent Georgian house in sixty acres of woodland just outside Haslemere: he could even see the golf course from his bedroom. Philip had been married for over twenty years and his wife Sally was chairman of the regional branch of the Save the Children Fund and a JP. Their son had just won a place at St Anne's College, Oxford.

Michael was the boy's godfather.

Michael Gilmour could not have been a greater contrast. On leaving school, where Philip had been his closest friend, he had drifted from job to job. He started out as a trainee with Watneys, but lasted only a few months before moving on to work as a rep with a publishing company. Like Philip, he married his childhood sweetheart, Carol West, the daughter of a local doctor.

When their own daughter was born, Carol complained about the hours Michael spent away from home so he left publishing and signed on as a distribution manager with a local soft drinks firm. He lasted for a couple of years until his deputy was promoted over him as area manager, at which decision Michael left in a huff. After his first spell on the dole, Michael joined a grain-packing company, but found he was allergic to corn and, having been supplied with a medical certificate to prove it, collected his first redundancy cheque. He then joined Philip as a Ready-Fit Kitchens rep but left without explanation within a month of the company being taken over. Another spell of unemployment followed before he took up the job of sales manager with a company that made microwave ovens. He seemed to have settled down at last until, without warning, he was made redundant. It was true that the company profits had been halved that year, while the company directors were sorry to see Michael go – or that was how it was expressed in their in-house magazine.

Carol was unable to hide her distress when Michael was made redundant for the fourth time. They could have done with the extra cash now that their daughter had been offered a place at art school.

Philip was the girl's godfather.

'What are you going to do about it?' asked Carol anxiously, when Michael had told her what had taken place at the club.

There's only one thing I can do,' he replied. 'After all, I have my reputation to consider. I shall sue the bastard.'

'That's a terrible way to talk about your oldest friend. And anyway we can't afford to go to law,' said Carol. 'Philip's a millionaire and we're penniless.'

'Can't be helped,' said Michael. 'I'll have to go through with it, even if it means selling up everything.'

'And even if the rest of your family has to suffer along with you?'

'None of us will suffer when he ends up paying my costs plus massive damages.'

'But you could *lose*,' said Carol. 'Then we would end up with nothing – worse than nothing.'

'That's not possible,' said Michael. 'He made the mistake of saying all those things in front of witnesses. There must have been over fifty members in the clubhouse this morning, including the president of the club and the editor of the local paper, and they couldn't have failed to hear every word.'

Carol remained unconvinced, and she was relieved that during the next few days Michael didn't mention Philip's name once. She hoped that her husband had come to his senses and the whole affair was best forgotten.

But then the *Haslemere Chronicle* decided to print its version of the quarrel between Michael and Philip. Under the headline 'Fight breaks out at golf club' came a carefully worded account of what had taken place on the previous Saturday. The editor of the *Haslemere Chronicle* knew only too well that the conversation itself was unprintable unless he also wanted to be sued, but he managed to include enough innuendo in the article to give a full flavour of what had happened that morning.

'That's the final straw,' said Michael, when he finished reading the article for a third time. Carol realised that nothing she could say or do was going to stop her husband now.

The following Monday, Michael contacted a local solicitor, Reginald Lomax, who had been at school with them both. Armed with the article, Michael briefed Lomax on the conversation that the *Chronicle* had felt injudicious to publish in any great detail.

Michael also gave Lomax his own detailed account of what had happened at the club that morning, and handed him four pages of handwritten notes to back his claims up.

Lomax studied the notes carefully.

'When did you write these?'

'In my car, immediately after we were suspended.'

'That was circumspect of you,' said Lomax. 'Most circumspect.' He stared quizzically at his client over the top of his half-moon spectacles. Michael made no comment. 'Of course you must be aware that the law is an expensive pastime,' Lomax continued. 'Suing for slander will not come cheap, and even with evidence as strong as this' – he tapped the notes in front of him – 'you could still lose. Slander depends so much on what other people remember or, more important, will admit to remembering.'

'I'm well aware of that,' said Michael. 'But I'm determined to go through with it. There were over fifty people in the club within earshot that morning.'

'So be it,' said Lomax. 'Then I shall require five thousand pounds in advance as a contingency fee to cover all the immediate costs and the preparations for a court case.' For the first time Michael looked hesitant.

'Returnable, of course, but only if you win the case.'

Michael removed his cheque book and wrote out a figure which, he reflected, would only just be covered by the remainder of his redundancy pay.

The writ for slander against Philip Masters was issued the next morning by Lomax, Davis and Lomax.

A week later the writ was accepted by another firm of solicitors in the same town, actually in the same building.

Back at the club, debate on the rights and wrongs of Gilmour v. Masters did not subside as the weeks passed.

Club members whispered furtively among themselves whether they might be called to give evidence at the trial. Several had already received letters from Lomax, Davis and Lomax requesting statements about what they could recall being said by the two men that morning. A good many pleaded amnesia or deafness but a few turned in graphic accounts of the quarrel. Encouraged, Michael pressed on, much to Carol's dismay.

One morning about a month later, after Carol had left for the bank, Michael Gilmour received a call from Reginald Lomax. The defendant's solicitors, he was informed, had requested a 'without prejudice' consultation.

'Surely you're not surprised by that after all the evidence we've collected?' Michael replied.

'It's only a consultation,' Lomax reminded him.

'Consultation or no consultation I won't settle for less than one hundred thousand pounds.'

'Well, I don't even know that they –' began Lomax.

'I do, and I also know that for the last eleven weeks I haven't been able to even get an interview for a job because of that bastard,' Michael said with contempt. 'Nothing less than one hundred thousand pounds, do you hear me?'

'I think you are being a trifle optimistic, in the circumstances,' said Lomax. 'But I'll call you and let you know the other side's response as soon as the meeting has taken place.'

Michael told Carol the good news that evening, but like Reginald Lomax she was sceptical. The ringing of the phone interrupted their discussion on the subject. Michael, with Carol standing by his side, listened carefully to Lomax's report. Philip, it seemed, was willing to settle for twenty-five thousand pounds and had agreed to paying both sides' costs.

Carol nodded her grateful acceptance, but Michael only repeated that Lomax was to hold out for nothing less than one hundred thousand. 'Can't you see that Philip's already worked out what it's going to cost him if this case ends up in court? And he knows only too well that I won't give in.'

Carol and Lomax remained unconvinced. 'It's much more touch and go than you realise,' the solicitor told him. 'A High Court jury might consider the words were only meant as banter.'

'Banter? But what about the fight that followed the banter?' said Michael.

'Started by you,' Lomax pointed out. 'Twenty-five thousand is a good figure in the circumstances,' he added.

Michael refused to budge, and ended the conversation by repeating his demand for one hundred thousand pounds.

Two weeks passed before the other side offered fifty thousand in exchange for a quick settlement. This time Lomax was not surprised when Michael rejected the offer out of hand. 'Quick settlement be damned. I've told you I won't consider less than a hundred thousand.' Lomax knew by now that any plea for prudence was going to fall on deaf ears.

It took three more weeks and several more phone calls between solicitors before the other side accepted that they were going to have to pay the full one hundred thousand pounds. Reginald Lomax rang Michael to inform him of the news late one evening, trying to make it sound as if he had scored a personal triumph. He assured Michael that the necessary papers could be drawn up immediately and the settlement signed in a matter of days.

'Naturally all your costs will be covered,' he added.

'Naturally,' said Michael.

'So all that is left for you to do now is agree on a statement.'

A short statement was penned and, with the agreement of both sides, issued to the *Haslemere Chronicle*. The paper printed the contents the following Friday on its front page. 'The writ for slander between Gilmour and Masters,' the *Chronicle* reported, 'has been withdrawn with the agreement of both sides but only after a substantial out-of-court settlement by the defendant. Philip Masters has withdrawn unreservedly what was said at the club that morning and has given an unconditional apology; he has also made a promise that he will never repeat the words used again. Mr Masters has paid the plaintiff's costs in full.'

Philip wrote to the Colonel the same day, admitting perhaps he had had a little too much to drink on the morning in question. He regretted his impetuous outburst, apologised and assured the club's president it would never happen again.

Carol was the only one who seemed to be saddened by the outcome.

'What's the matter, darling?' asked Michael. 'We've won, and what's more it's solved our financial problems.'

'I know,' said Carol, 'but is it worth losing your closest friend for one hundred thousand pounds?'

On the following Saturday morning Michael was pleased to find an envelope among his morning post with the Golf Club crest on the flap. He opened it nervously and pulled out a single sheet of paper. It read:

Dear Mr Gilmour,
    At the monthly committee meeting held last Wednesday Colonel Mather raised the matter of

your behaviour in the clubhouse on the morning of Saturday, April 16th.

It was decided to minute the complaints of several members, but on this occasion only to issue a severe reprimand to you both. Should a similar incident occur in the future, loss of membership would be automatic.

The temporary suspension issued by Colonel Mather on April 16th is now lifted.

Yours sincerely,

Jeremy Howard

Jeremy Howard (Secretary)

'I'm off to do the shopping,' shouted Carol from the top of the stairs. 'What are your plans for the morning?'

'I'm going to have a round of golf,' said Michael, folding up the letter.

'Good idea,' said Carol to herself as she wondered whom Michael would find to play against in the future.

Quite a few members noticed Michael and Philip teeing up at the first hole that Saturday morning. The club captain commented to the Colonel that he was glad to observe that the quarrel had been sorted out to everyone's satisfaction.

'Not to mine,' said the Colonel under his breath. 'You can't get drunk on tomato juice.'

'I wonder what the devil they can be talking about?' the club captain said as he stared at them both through the bay windows. The Colonel raised his binoculars to take a closer look at the two men.

'How could you possibly miss a four-foot putt, dummy?' asked Michael when they had reached the first green. 'You must be drunk again.'

'As you well know,' replied Philip, 'I never drink before dinner, and I therefore suggest that your allegation that I am drunk again is nothing less than slander.'

'Yes, but where are your witnesses?' said Michael as they moved up on to the second tee. 'I had over fifty, don't forget.'

Both men laughed.

Their conversation ranged over many subjects as they played the first eight holes, never once touching on their past quarrel until they reached the ninth green, the farthest point from the clubhouse. They both checked to see there was no one within earshot. The nearest player was still putting out some two hundred yards behind them on the eighth hole. It was then that Michael removed a bulky brown envelope from his golf bag and handed it over to Philip.

'Thank you,' said Philip, dropping the package into his own golf bag as he removed a putter. 'As neat a little operation as I've been involved in for a long time,' Philip added as he addressed the ball.

'I end up with forty thousand pounds,' said Michael grinning, 'while you lose nothing at all.'

'Only because I pay tax at the highest rate and can therefore claim the loss as a legitimate business expense,' said Philip, 'and I wouldn't have been able to do that if I hadn't once employed you.'

'And I, as a successful litigant, need pay no tax at all on damages received in a civil case.'

'A loophole that even this Chancellor hasn't caught on to,' said Philip.

'Even though it went to Reggie Lomax, I was sorry about the solicitors' fees,' added Michael.

'No problem, old fellow. They're also one hundred per cent claimable against tax. So as you see, I didn't lose a penny and you ended up with forty thousand pounds tax free.'

'And nobody the wiser,' said Michael, laughing.

The Colonel put his binoculars back into their case.

'Had your eye on this year's winner of the President's Putter, Colonel?' asked the club captain.

'No,' the Colonel replied. 'The certain sponsor of this year's Youth Tournament.'

CHRISTINA ROSENTHAL

THE RABBI KNEW he couldn't hope to begin on his sermon until he'd read the letter. He had been sitting at his desk in front of a blank sheet of paper for over an hour and still couldn't come up with a first sentence. Lately he had been unable to concentrate on a task he had carried out every Friday evening for the last thirty years. They must have realised by now that he was no longer up to it. He took the letter out of the envelope and slowly unfolded the pages. Then he pushed his half-moon spectacles up the bridge of his nose and started to read.

My dear Father,

'Jew boy! Jew boy! Jew boy!' were the first words I ever heard her say as I ran past her on the first lap of the race. She was standing behind the railing at the beginning of the home straight, hands cupped around her lips to be sure I couldn't miss the chant. She must have come from another school because I didn't recognise her, but it only took a fleeting glance to see that it was Greg Reynolds who was standing by her side.

After five years of having to tolerate his snide comments and bullying at school all I wanted to retaliate with was, 'Nazi,

Nazi, Nazi,' but you had always taught me to rise above such provocation.

I tried to put them both out of my mind as I moved into the second lap. I had dreamed for years of winning the mile in the West Mount High School championships, and I was determined not to let them do anything to stop me.

As I came into the back straight a second time I took a more careful look at her. She was standing amid a cluster of friends who were wearing the scarves of Marianapolis Convent. She must have been about sixteen, and as slim as a willow. I wonder if you would have chastised me had I only shouted, 'No breasts, no breasts, no breasts.' in the hope it might at least provoke the boy standing next to her into a fight. Then I would have been able to tell you truthfully that he had thrown the first punch but the moment you had learned that it was Greg Reynolds you would have realised how little provocation I needed.

As I reached the back straight I once again prepared myself for the chants. Chanting at track meetings had become fashionable in the late 1950s when 'Zat-o-pek, Zat-o-pek, Zat-o-pek' had been roared in adulation across running stadiums around the world for the great Czech champion. Not for me was there to be the shout of 'Ros-en-thal, Ros-en-thal, Ros-en-thal' as I came into earshot.

'Jew boy! Jew boy! Jew boy!' she said, sounding like a gramophone record that had got stuck. Her friend Greg, who would nowadays be described as a preppie, began laughing. I knew he had put her up to it, and how I would like to have removed that smug grin from his face. I reached the half-mile mark in two minutes seventeen seconds, comfortably inside the

pace necessary to break the school record, and I felt that was the best way to put the taunting girl and that fascist Reynolds in their place. I couldn't help thinking at the time how unfair it all was. I was a real Canadian, born and bred in this country, while she was just an immigrant. After all, you, Father, had escaped from Hamburg in 1937 and started with nothing. Her parents did not land on these shores until 1949, by which time you were a respected figure in the community.

I gritted my teeth and tried to concentrate. Zatopek had written in his autobiography that no runner can afford to lose his concentration during a race. When I reached the penultimate bend the inevitable chanting began again, but this time it only made me speed up and even more determined to break that record. Once I was back in the safety of the home straight I could hear some of my friends roaring, 'Come on, Benjamin, you can do it,' and the timekeeper called out, 'Three twenty-three, three twenty-four, three twenty-five' as I passed the bell to begin the last lap.

I knew that the record – four thirty-two – was now well within my grasp and all those dark nights of winter training suddenly seemed worthwhile. As I reached the back straight I took the lead, and even felt that I could face the girl again. I summoned up my strength for one last effort. A quick glance over my shoulder confirmed I was already yards in front of any of my rivals, so it was only me against the clock. Then I heard the chanting, but this time it was even louder than before, 'Jew boy! Jew boy! Jew boy!' It was louder because the two of them were now working in unison, and just as I came round the bend Reynolds raised his arm in a flagrant Nazi salute.

If I had only carried on for another twenty yards I would

have reached the safety of the home straight and the cheers of my friends, the cup and the record. But they had made me so angry that I could no longer control myself.

I shot off the track and ran across the grass over the long-jump pit and straight towards them. At least my crazy decision stopped their chanting because Reynolds lowered his arm and just stood there staring pathetically at me from behind the small railing that surrounded the outer perimeter of the track. I leaped right over it and landed in front of my adversary. With all the energy I had saved for the final straight I took an almighty swing at him. My fist landed an inch below his left eye and he buckled and fell to the ground by her side. Quickly she knelt down and, staring up, gave me a look of such hatred that no words could have matched it. Once I was sure Greg wasn't going to get up, I walked slowly back on to the track as the last of the runners were coming round the final bend.

'Last again, Jew boy,' I heard her shout as I jogged down the home straight, so far behind the others that they didn't even bother to record my time.

How often since have you quoted me those words: 'Still have I borne it with a patient shrug, for sufferance is the badge of all our tribe'. Of course you were right, but I was only seventeen then, and even after I had learned the truth about Christina's father I still couldn't understand how anyone who had come from a defeated Germany, a Germany condemned by the rest of the world for its treatment of the Jews, could still behave in such a manner. And in those days I really believed her family were Nazis, but I remember you patiently explaining to me that her father had been an admiral in the German navy, and had won an Iron Cross for sinking Allied ships. Do you remember me asking how could you tolerate such a man, let alone allow him to settle down in our country?

You went on to assure me that Admiral von Braumer, who came from an old Roman Catholic family and probably despised the Nazis as much as we did, had acquitted himself honourably as an officer and a gentleman throughout his life as a German sailor. But I still couldn't accept your attitude, or didn't want to.

It didn't help, Father, that you always saw the other man's point of view, and even though Mother had died prematurely because of those bastards you could still find it in you to forgive.

If you had been born a Christian, you would have been a saint.

The rabbi put the letter down and rubbed his tired eyes before he turned over another page written in that fine script that he had taught his only son so many years before. Benjamin had always learned quickly, everything from the Hebrew scriptures to a complicated algebraic equation. The old man had even begun to hope the boy might become a rabbi.

Do you remember my asking you that evening why people couldn't understand that the world had changed? Didn't the girl realise that she was no better than we were? I shall never forget your reply. She is, you said, far better than us, if the only way you can prove your superiority is to punch her friend in the face.

I returned to my room angered by your weakness. It was to be many years before I understood your strength.

When I wasn't pounding round that track I rarely had time

for anything other than working for a scholarship to McGill, so it came as a surprise that her path crossed mine again so soon.

It must have been about a week later that I saw her at the local swimming pool. She was standing at the deep end, just under the diving board, when I came in. Her long fair hair was dancing on her shoulders, her bright eyes eagerly taking in everything going on around her. Greg was by her side. I was pleased to notice a deep purple patch remained under his left eye for all to see. I also remember chuckling to myself because she really did have the flattest chest I had ever seen on a sixteen-year-old girl, though I have to confess she had fantastic legs. Perhaps she's a freak, I thought. I turned to go in to the changing room – a split second before I hit the water. When I came up for breath there was no sign of who had pushed me in, just a group of grinning but innocent faces. I didn't need a law degree to work out who it must have been, but as you constantly reminded me, Father, without evidence there is no proof . . . I wouldn't have minded that much about being pushed into the pool if I hadn't been wearing my best suit – in truth, my only suit with long trousers, the one I wore on days I was going to the synagogue.

I climbed out of the water but didn't waste any time looking round for him. I knew Greg would be a long way off by then. I walked home through the back streets, avoiding taking the bus in case someone saw me and told you what a state I was in. As soon as I got home I crept past your study and on upstairs to my room, changing before you had the chance to discover what had taken place.

Old Isaac Cohen gave me a disapproving look when I turned up at the synagogue an hour later wearing a blazer and jeans.

I took the suit to the cleaners the next morning. It cost me three weeks' pocket money to be sure that you were never aware of what had happened at the swimming pool that day.

The rabbi picked up the picture of his seventeen-year-old son in that synagogue suit. He well remembered Benjamin turning up to his service in a blazer and jeans and Isaac Cohen's outspoken reprimand. The rabbi was thankful that Mr Atkins, the swimming instructor, had phoned to warn him of what had taken place that afternoon so at least he didn't add to Mr Cohen's harsh words. He continued gazing at the photograph for a long time before he returned to the letter.

The next occasion I saw Christina – by now I had found out her name – was at the end-of-term dance held in the school gymnasium. I thought I looked pretty cool in my neatly pressed suit until I saw Greg standing by her side in a smart new dinner jacket. I remember wondering at the time if I would ever be able to afford a dinner jacket. Greg had been offered a place at McGill and was announcing the fact to everyone who cared to listen, which made me all the more determined to win a scholarship there the following year.

I stared at Christina. She was wearing a long red dress that completely covered those beautiful legs. A thin gold belt emphasised her tiny waist and the only jewellery she wore was a simple gold necklace. I knew if I waited a moment longer I wouldn't have the courage to go through with it. I clenched my fists, walked over to where they were sitting, and as you had always taught me, Father, bowed slightly before I asked, 'May I have the pleasure of this dance?'

She stared into my eyes. I swear if she had told me to go out and kill a thousand men before I dared ask her again I would have done it.

She didn't even speak, but Greg leaned over her shoulder and said, 'Why don't you go and find yourself a nice Jewish girl?' I thought I saw her scowl at his remark, but I only blushed like someone who's been caught with their hands in the cookie jar. I didn't dance with anyone that night. I walked straight out of the gymnasium and ran home.

I was convinced then that I hated her.

That last week of term I broke the school record for the mile. You were there to watch me but, thank heavens, she wasn't. That was the holiday we drove over to Ottawa to spend our summer vacation with Aunt Rebecca. I was told by a school friend that Christina had spent hers in Vancouver with a German family. At least Greg had not gone with her, the friend assured me.

You went on reminding me of the importance of a good education, but you didn't need to, because every time I saw Greg it made me more determined to win that scholarship.

I worked even harder in the summer of '65 when you explained that, for a Canadian, a place at McGill was like going to Harvard or Oxford and would clear a path for the rest of my days.

For the first time in my life running took second place.

Although I didn't see much of Christina that term she was often in my mind. A classmate told me that she and Greg were no longer seeing each other, but could give me no reason for this sudden change of heart. At the time I had a so-called girlfriend who always sat on the other side of the synagogue – Naomi Goldblatz, you remember her – but it was she who dated me.

As my exams drew nearer, I was grateful that you always found time to go over my essays and tests after I had finished them. What you couldn't know was that I inevitably returned to my own room to do them a third time. Often I would fall asleep at my desk. When I woke I would turn over the page and read on.

Even you, Father, who have not an ounce of vanity in you, found it hard to disguise from your congregation the pride you took in my eight straight 'A's' and the award of a top scholarship to McGill. I wondered if Christina was aware of it. She must have been. My name was painted up on the Honours Board in fresh gold leaf the following week, so someone would have told her.

It must have been three months later when I was in my first term at McGill that I saw her next. Do you remember taking me to St Joan at the Centaur Theatre? There she was, seated a few rows in front of us with her parents and a sophomore called Bob Richards. The admiral and his wife looked strait-laced and very stern but not unsympathetic. In the interval I watched her laughing and joking with them: she had obviously enjoyed herself. I hardly saw St Joan, and although I couldn't take my eyes off Christina she never once noticed me. I just wanted to be on the stage playing the Dauphin so she would have to look up at me.

When the curtain came down she and Bob Richards left her

parents and headed for the exit. I followed the two of them out of the foyer and into the car park, and watched them get into a Thunderbird. A Thunderbird! I remember thinking I might one day be able to afford a dinner jacket, but never a Thunderbird.

From that moment she was in my thoughts whenever I trained, wherever I worked and even when I slept. I found out everything I could about Bob Richards and discovered that he was liked by all who knew him.

For the first time in my life I hated being a Jew.

When I next saw Christina I dreaded what might happen. It was the start of the mile against the University of Vancouver and as a freshman I had been lucky to be selected for McGill. When I came out on to the track to warm up I saw her sitting in the third row of the stand alongside Richards. They were holding hands.

I was last off when the starter's gun fired but as we went into the back straight moved up into fifth position. It was the largest crowd I had ever run in front of, and when I reached the home straight I waited for the chant 'Jew boy! Jew boy! Jew boy!' but nothing happened. I wondered if she had failed to notice that I was in the race. But she had noticed because as I came round the bend I could hear her voice clearly. 'Come on, Benjamin, you've got to win!' she shouted.

I wanted to look back to make sure it was Christina who had called those words; it would be another quarter of a mile before I could pass her again. By the time I did so I had moved up into third place, and I could hear her clearly: 'Come on, Benjamin, you can do it!'

I immediately took the lead because all I wanted to do was get back to her. I charged on without thought of who was behind me, and by the time I passed her the third time I was several yards ahead of the field. 'You're going to win!' she shouted as I ran on to reach the bell in three minutes eight seconds, eleven seconds faster than I had ever done before. I remember thinking that they ought to put something in those training manuals about love being worth two to three seconds a lap.

I watched her all the way down the back straight and when I came into the final bend for the last time the crowd rose to their feet. I turned to search for her. She was jumping up and down shouting, 'Look out! Look out!' which I didn't understand until I was overtaken on the inside by the Vancouver Number One string who the coach had warned me was renowned for his strong finish. I staggered over the line a few yards behind him in second place but went on running until I was safely inside the changing room. I sat alone by my locker. Four minutes seventeen, someone told me: six seconds faster than I had ever run before. It didn't help. I stood in the shower for a long time, trying to work out what could possibly have changed her attitude.

When I walked back on to the track only the ground staff were still around. I took one last look at the finishing line before I strolled over to the Forsyth Library. I felt unable to face the usual team get-together, so I tried to settle down to write an essay on the property rights of married women.

The library was almost empty that Saturday evening and I was well into my third page when I heard a voice say, 'I hope I'm not interrupting you but you didn't come to Joe's.' I looked up to see Christina standing on the other side of the table. Father, I didn't know what to say. I just stared up at the beautiful creature in her fashionable blue mini-skirt and tight-fitting sweater that emphasised the most perfect breasts, and said nothing.

'I was the one who shouted "Jew boy" when you were still at High School. I've felt ashamed about it ever since. I wanted to apologise to you on the night of the prom dance but couldn't summon up the courage with Greg standing there.' I nodded my understanding – couldn't think of any words that seemed appropriate. 'I never spoke to him again,' she said. 'But I don't suppose you even remember Greg.'

I just smiled. 'Care for coffee?' I asked, trying to sound as if I wouldn't mind if she replied, 'I'm sorry, I must get back to Bob.'

'I'd like that very much,' she said.

I took her to the library coffee shop, which was about all I could afford at the time. She never bothered to explain what had happened to Bob Richards, and I never asked.

Christina seemed to know so much about me that I felt embarrassed. She asked me to forgive her for what she had shouted on the track that day two years before. She made no excuses, placed the blame on no one else, just asked to be forgiven.

Christina told me she was hoping to join me at McGill in September, to major in German. 'Bit of a cheek,' she admitted, 'as it is my native tongue.'

We spent the rest of that summer in each other's company. We saw St Joan again, and even queued for a film called Dr No that was all the craze at the time. We worked together, we ate together, we played together, but we slept alone.

I said little about Christina to you at the time, but I'd bet you knew already how much I loved her; I could never hide anything from you. And after all your teaching of forgiveness and understanding you could hardly disapprove.

The rabbi paused. His heart ached because he knew so much of what was still to come although he could not have foretold what would happen in the end. He had never thought he would live to regret his Orthodox upbringing but when Mrs Goldblatz first told him about Christina he had been unable to mask his disapproval. It will pass, given time, he told her. So much for wisdom.

Whenever I went to Christina's home I was always treated with courtesy but her family were unable to hide their disapproval. They uttered words they didn't believe in an attempt to show that they were not anti-semitic, and whenever I brought up the subject with Christina she told me I was over-reacting. We both knew I wasn't. They quite simply thought I was unworthy of their daughter. They were right, but it had nothing to do with my being Jewish.

I shall never forget the first time we made love. It was the day that Christina learned she had won a place at McGill.

We had gone to my room at three o'clock to change for a game of tennis. I took her in my arms for what I thought would be a brief moment and we didn't part until the next morning. Nothing had been planned. But how could it have been, when it was the first time for both of us?

I told her I would marry her – don't all men the first time? – only I meant it.

Then a few weeks later she missed her period. I begged her not to panic, and we both waited for another month because she was fearful of going to see any doctor in Montreal.

If I had told you everything then, Father, perhaps my life would have taken a different course. But I didn't, and have only myself to blame.

I began to plan for a marriage that neither Christina's family nor you could possibly have found acceptable, but we didn't care. Love knows no parents, and certainly no religion. When she missed her second period I agreed Christina should tell her mother. I asked her if she would like me to be with her at the time, but she simply shook her head, and explained that she felt she had to face them on her own.

'I'll wait here until you return,' I promised.

She smiled. 'I'll be back even before you've had the time to change your mind about marrying me.'

I sat in my room at McGill all that afternoon reading and pacing – mostly pacing – but she never came back, and I didn't go in search of her until it was dark. I crept round to her home, all the while trying to convince myself there must be some simple explanation as to why she hadn't returned.

When I reached her road I could see a light on in her bedroom but nowhere else in the house so I thought she must be alone. I marched through the gate and up to the front porch, knocked on the door and waited.

Her father answered the door.

'What do you want?' he asked, his eyes never leaving me for a moment.

'I love your daughter,' I told him, 'and I want to marry her.'

'*She will never marry a Jew,*' *he said simply and closed the door. I remember that he didn't slam it; he just closed it, which made it somehow even worse.*

I stood outside in the road staring up at her room for over an hour until the light went out. Then I walked home. I recall there was a light drizzle that night and few people were on the streets. I tried to work out what I should do next, although the situation seemed hopeless to me. I went to bed that night hoping for a miracle. I had forgotten that miracles are for Christians, not Jews.

By the next morning I had worked out a plan. I phoned Christina's home at eight and nearly put the phone down when I heard the voice at the other end.

'*Mrs von Braumer,*' *she said.*

'*Is Christina there?*' *I asked in a whisper.*

'*No, she's not,*' *came back the controlled impersonal reply.*

'*When are you expecting her back?*' *I asked.*

'*Not for some time,*' *she said, and then the phone went dead.*

'*Not for some time*' *turned out to be over a year. I wrote, telephoned, asked friends from school and university but could never find out where they had taken her.*

Then one day, unannounced, she returned to Montreal accompanied by a husband and my child. I learned the bitter details from that font of all knowledge, Naomi Goldblatz, who had already seen all three of them.

I received a short note from Christina about a week later begging me not to make any attempt to contact her.

I had just begun my last year at McGill and like some eighteenth-century gentleman I honoured her wish to the letter and turned all my energies to the final exams. She still continued to preoccupy my thoughts and I considered myself lucky at the end of the year to be offered a place at Harvard Law School.

I left Montreal for Boston on September 12th, 1968.

You must have wondered why I never came home once during those three years. I knew of your disapproval. Thanks to Mrs Goldblatz everyone was aware who the father of Christina's child was and I felt an enforced absence might make life a little easier for you.

The rabbi paused as he remembered Mrs Goldblatz letting him know what she had considered was 'only her duty'.

'You're an interfering old busybody,' he had told her. By the following Saturday she had moved to another synagogue and let everyone in the town know why.

He was more angry with himself than with Benjamin. He should have visited Harvard to let his son know that his love for him had not changed. So much for his powers of forgiveness.

He took up the letter once again.

Throughout those years at law school I had plenty of friends of both sexes, but Christina was rarely out of my mind for more than a few hours at a time. I wrote over forty letters to her while I was in Boston, but didn't post one of them. I even phoned, but it was never her voice that answered. If it had been, I'm not even sure I would have said anything. I just wanted to hear her.

Were you ever curious about the women in my life? I had

affairs with bright girls from Radcliffe who were reading law, history or science, and once with a shop assistant who never read anything. Can you imagine, in the very act of making love, always thinking of another woman? I seemed to be doing my work on autopilot, and even my passion for running became reduced to an hour's jogging a day.

Long before the end of my last year, leading law firms in New York, Chicago and Toronto were turning up to interview us. The Harvard tom-toms can be relied on to beat across the world, but even I was surprised by a visit from the senior partner of Graham Douglas & Wilkins of Toronto. It's not a firm known for its Jewish partners, but I liked the idea of their letterhead one day reading 'Graham Douglas Wilkins & Rosenthal'. Even her father would surely have been impressed by that.

At least if I lived and worked in Toronto, I convinced myself, it would be far enough away for me to forget her, and perhaps with luck find someone else I could feel that way about.

Graham Douglas & Wilkins found me a spacious apartment overlooking the park and started me off at a handsome salary. In return I worked all the hours God – whoever's God – made. If I thought they had pushed me at McGill or Harvard, Father, it turned out to be no more than a dry run for the real world. I didn't complain. The work was exciting, and the rewards beyond my expectation. Only now that I could afford a Thunderbird I didn't want one.

New girlfriends came, and went as soon as they talked of marriage. The Jewish ones usually raised the subject within a week, the Gentiles, I found, waited a little longer. I even began living with one of them, Rebecca Wertz, but that too ended – on a Thursday.

I was driving to the office that morning – it must have been a little after eight, which was late for me – when I saw Christina on the other side of the busy highway, a barrier separating us. She was standing at a bus stop holding the hand of a little boy, who must have been about five – my son.

The heavy morning traffic allowed me a little longer to stare in disbelief. I found that I wanted to look at them both at once. She wore a long lightweight coat that showed she had not lost her figure. Her face was serene and only reminded me why she was rarely out of my thoughts. Her son – our son – was wrapped up in an oversize duffle coat and his head was covered by a baseball hat that informed me that he supported the Toronto Dolphins. Sadly, it really stopped me seeing what he looked like. You can't be in Toronto, I remember thinking, you're meant to be in Montreal. I watched them both in my side-mirror as they climbed on to a bus. That particular Thursday I must have been an appalling counsellor to every client who sought my advice.

For the next week I passed by that bus stop every morning within minutes of the time I had seen them standing there but never saw them again. I began to wonder if I had imagined the whole scene. Then I spotted Christina again when I was returning across the city, having visited a client. She was on her own and I braked hard as I watched her entering a shop on Bloor Street. This time I double-parked the car and walked quickly across the road feeling like a sleazy private detective who spends his life peeping through keyholes.

What I saw took me by surprise – not to find her in a beautiful dress shop, but to discover it was where she worked.

The moment I saw that she was serving a customer I

*hurried back to my car. Once I had reached my office I asked
my secretary if she knew of a shop called 'Willing's'.*

*My secretary laughed. 'You must pronounce it the German
way, the W becomes a V,' she explained, 'thus Villing's'. If you
were married you would know that it's the most expensive dress
shop in town,' she added.*

*'Do you know anything else about the place?' I asked, trying
to sound casual.*

*'Not a lot,' she said. 'Only that it is owned by a wealthy
German lady called Mrs Klaus Willing whom they often write
about in the women's magazines.'*

*I didn't need to ask my secretary any more questions and I
won't trouble you, Father, with my detective work. But, armed
with those snippets of information, it didn't take me long to
discover where Christina lived, that her husband was an overseas
director with BMW, and that they only had the one child.*

The old rabbi breathed deeply as he glanced up at
the clock on his desk, more out of habit than any
desire to know the time. He paused for a moment
before returning to the letter. He had been so proud
of his lawyer son then; why hadn't he made the first
step towards a reconciliation? How he would have
liked to have seen his grandson.

*My ultimate decision did not require an acute legal mind, just a
little common sense – although a lawyer who advises himself
undoubtedly has a fool for a client. Contact, I decided, had to
be direct and a letter was the only method I felt Christina would
find acceptable.*

I wrote a simple message that Monday morning, then rewrote it several times before I telephoned 'Fleet Deliveries' and asked them to hand it to her in person at the shop. When the young man left with the letter I wanted to follow him, just to be certain he had given it to the right person. I can still repeat it word for word.

Dear Christina,
> *You must know I live and work in Toronto. Can we meet? I will wait for you in the lounge of the Royal York Hotel every evening between six and seven this week. If you don't come be assured I will never trouble you again.*

Benjamin

I arrived that evening nearly thirty minutes early. I remember taking a seat in a large impersonal lounge just off the main hall and ordering coffee.

'Will anyone be joining you, sir?' the waiter asked.

'I can't be sure,' I told him. No one did join me, but I still hung around until seven forty.

By Thursday the waiter had stopped asking if anyone would be joining me as I sat alone and allowed yet another cup of coffee to grow cold. Every few minutes I checked my watch. Each time a woman with blonde hair entered the lounge my heart leaped but it was never the woman I hoped for.

It was just before seven on Friday that I finally saw Christina standing in the doorway. She wore a smart blue suit buttoned up almost to the neck and a white blouse that made her look as if she were on her way to a business conference. Her long fair hair was pulled back behind her ears to give an impression of severity, but however hard she tried she could not be other than beautiful. I stood and raised my arm. She walked quickly over and took the seat beside me. We didn't kiss or shake hands and for some time didn't even speak.

'Thank you for coming,' I said.

'I shouldn't have, it was foolish.'

Some time passed before either of us spoke again.

'Can I pour you a coffee?' I asked.

'Yes, thank you.'

'Black?'

'Yes.'

'You haven't changed.'

How banal it all would have sounded to anyone eavesdropping.

She sipped her coffee.

I should have taken her in my arms right then but I had no way of knowing that that was what she wanted. For several minutes we talked of inconsequential matters, always avoiding each other's eyes, until I suddenly said, 'Do you realise that I still love you?'

Tears filled her eyes as she replied, 'Of course I do. And I still feel the same about you now as I did the day we parted. And don't forget I have to see you every day, through Nicholas.'

She leaned forward and spoke almost in a whisper. She told me about the meeting with her parents that had taken place more than five years before as if we had not been parted in between. Her father had shown no anger when he learned she was pregnant but the family still left for Vancouver the following morning. There they had stayed with the Willings, a family also from Munich, who were old friends of the von Braumers. Their son, Klaus, had always been besotted with Christina and didn't care about her being pregnant, or even the fact she felt nothing for him. He was confident that, given time, it would all work out for the best.

It didn't, because it couldn't. Christina had always known it would never work, however hard Klaus tried. They even left Montreal in an attempt to make a go of it. Klaus bought her the shop in Toronto and every luxury that money could afford, but it made no difference. Their marriage was an obvious sham. Yet they could not bring themselves to distress their families further with a divorce so they had led separate lives from the beginning.

As soon as Christina finished her story I touched her cheek and she took my hand and kissed it. From that moment on we saw each other every spare moment that could be stolen, day or night. It was the happiest year of my life, and I was unable to hide from anyone how I felt.

Our affair – for that's how the gossips were describing it – inevitably became public. However discreet we tried to be, Toronto, I quickly discovered, is a very small place, full of people who took pleasure in informing those whom we also loved that we had been seen together regularly, even leaving my home in the early hours.

Then quite suddenly we were left with no choice in the matter: Christina told me she was pregnant again. Only this time it held no fears for either of us.

Once she had told Klaus the settlement went through as quickly as the best divorce lawyer at Graham Douglas & Wilkins could negotiate. We were married only a few days after the final papers were signed. We both regretted that Christina's parents felt unable to attend the wedding but I couldn't understand why you didn't come.

The rabbi still could not believe his own intolerance and short-sightedness. The demands on an Orthodox Jew should be waived if it meant losing one's only child. He had searched the Talmud in vain for any passage that would allow him to break his lifelong vows. In vain.

The only sad part of the divorce settlement was that Klaus was given custody of our child. He also demanded, in exchange for a quick divorce, that I not be allowed to see Nicholas before his twenty-first birthday, and that he should not be told that I was his real father. At the time it seemed a hard price to pay, even for such happiness. We both knew that we had been left with no choice but to accept his terms.

I used to wonder how each day could be so much better than the last. If I was apart from Christina for more than a few hours I always missed her. If the firm sent me out of town on business for a night I would phone her two, three, perhaps four times, and if it was for more than a night then she came with me. I remember you once describing your love for my mother and wondering at the time if I could ever hope to achieve such happiness.

We began to make plans for the birth of our child. William, if it was a boy – her choice; Deborah, if it was a girl – mine. I painted the spare room pink, assuming I had already won.

Christina had to stop me buying too many baby clothes, but I warned her that it didn't matter as we were going to have a dozen more children. Jews, I reminded her, believed in dynasties.

She attended her exercise classes regularly, dieted carefully, rested sensibly. I told her she was doing far more than was required of a mother, even of my daughter. I asked if I could be present when our child was born and her gynaecologist seemed reluctant at first, but then agreed. By the time the ninth month came the hospital must have thought from the amount of fuss I was making they were preparing for the birth of a royal prince.

I drove Christina into Women's College Hospital on the way to work last Tuesday. Although I went on to the office I found it impossible to concentrate. The hospital rang in the afternoon to say they thought the child would be born early that evening: obviously Deborah did not wish to disrupt the working hours of Graham Douglas & Wilkins. However, I still arrived at the hospital far too early. I sat on the end of Christina's bed until her contractions started coming every minute and then to my surprise they asked me to leave. They needed to rupture her membranes, a nurse explained. I asked her to remind the midwife that I wanted to be present to witness the birth.

I went out into the corridor and began pacing up and down, the way expectant fathers do in B-movies. Christina's gynaecologist arrived about half an hour later and gave me a huge smile. I noticed a cigar in his top pocket, obviously reserved for expectant fathers. 'It's about to happen,' was all he said.

A second doctor whom I had never seen before arrived a few minutes later and went quickly into her room. He only gave me a nod. I felt like a man in the dock waiting to hear the jury's verdict.

It must have been at least another fifteen minutes before I saw the unit being rushed down the corridor by a team of three *young interns. They didn't even give me so much as a second glance as they disappeared into Christina's room.*

I heard the screams that suddenly gave way to the plaintive cry of a new-born child. I thanked my God and hers. When the doctor came out of her room I remember noticing that the cigar had disappeared.

'It's a girl,' he said quietly. I was overjoyed. 'No need to repaint the bedroom immediately' flashed through my mind.

'Can I see Christina now?' I asked.

He took me by the arm and led me across the corridor and into his office.

'Would you like to sit down?' he asked. 'I'm afraid I have some sad news.'

'Is she all right?'

'I am sorry, so very sorry, to tell you that your wife is dead.'

At first I didn't believe him, I refused to believe him. Why? Why? I wanted to scream.

'We did warn her,' he added.

'Warn her? Warn her of what?'

'That her blood pressure might not stand up to it a second time.'

Christina had never told me what the doctor went on to explain – that the birth of our first child had been complicated, and that the doctors had advised her against becoming pregnant again.

'Why hadn't she told me?' I demanded. Then I realised why. She had risked everything for me – foolish, selfish, thoughtless me – and I had ended up killing the one person I loved.

They allowed me to hold Deborah in my arms for just a moment before they put her into an incubator and told me it would be another twenty-four hours before she came off the danger list.

You will never know how much it meant to me, Father, that you came to the hospital so quickly. Christina's parents arrived later that evening. They were magnificent. He begged for my forgiveness — begged for my forgiveness. It could never have happened, he kept repeating, if he hadn't been so stupid and prejudiced.

His wife took my hand and asked if she might be allowed to see Deborah from time to time. Of course I agreed. They left just before midnight. I sat, walked, slept in that corridor for the next twenty-four hours until they told me that my daughter was off the danger list. She would have to remain in the hospital for a few more days, they explained, but she was now managing to suck milk from a bottle.

Christina's father kindly took over the funeral arrangements.

You must have wondered why I didn't appear and I owe you an explanation. I thought I would just drop into the hospital on my way to the funeral so that I could spend a few moments with Deborah. I had already transferred my love.

The doctor couldn't get the words out. It took a brave man to tell me that her heart had stopped beating a few minutes before my arrival. Even the senior surgeon was in tears. When I left the hospital the corridors were empty.

I want you to know, Father, that I love you with all my heart, but I have no desire to spend the rest of my life without Christina or Deborah.

I only ask to be buried beside my wife and daughter and to

be remembered as their husband and father. That way unthinking people might learn from our love. And when you finish this letter, remember only that I had such total happiness when I was with her that death holds no fears for me.

    Your son,
        Benjamin.

The old rabbi placed the letter down on the table in front of him. He had read it every day for the last ten years.